Erwin's Law

§

An Erwin Tennyson Mystery

Si Dunn

Published by
Sagecreek Productions, LLC
Austin, Texas

For Carmen, who muses and amuses.

ISBN-13: 978-0-985-1735-5-5

Publishing history:
Second edition (paperback)
First edition (FictionWorks e-book)

ONE

The detective looked up from his small notepad. "What's your occupation, Mister Tennyson?"

"Mostly, I'm retired," I said.

The Austin police detective was tall, lean, blond. His casual clothes fit him perfectly and were clean and unwrinkled.

I wondered if he was making notes about my description: medium height; pudgy gut; thinning white hair, pasty complexion; soft-muscled. *A man who spends too much time reading books and sitting at computers.*

I glanced at my watch. Just thirty minutes ago, I decided to jog, my first run in perhaps fifteen years. Three minutes into it, gasping and wheezing, I veered off the park path into some bushes. I wanted to rest in some shade.

Instead, I stumbled over a body.

"So you work part-time," the detective said.

I nodded, stalling. What I did was not many people's definition of "work."

He looked at me, waiting for more.

"I write book reviews for the *Daily Democrat*," I said.

"Book reviews."

"Detective novels, mostly."

"Detective novels." The detective smirked as he wrote this down.

Nearby, two crime scene investigators clicked their digital cameras as they moved carefully around the death scene and near the body.

A woman who appeared to be Hispanic and in her late twenties was lying face up. A bullet hole was centered in her forehead.

"Anything else come to mind?" The young detective seemed ready to close his notepad.

I wanted to say yes. Something about the victim did seem vaguely familiar.

Austin prided itself on being a major city, yet it was still small enough that you could keep running across people you had seen before.

But *had* I seen the victim before? And where?

Library? Mall? Restaurant? Coffee shop? I almost never went to bars.

My vague feeling added up to nothing he could write down. I shook my head no.

He pulled a police business card from his shirt pocket. "If you think of something, give me a call."

I glanced at the card: "Det. Sgt. Paul Marklin, Jr." I looked at it again.

"Your Dad was a Texas Ranger," I said.

Sgt. Marklin grinned. "Thirty-two years."

"I reviewed his book after he retired."

"*Danger Ranger*." He's writing another novel now about the Rangers."

Behind us, a voice called out, "Sergeant Marklin?" We looked around.

One of the CSIs gestured at two short, muscular emergency medical technicians. They were now standing ready to bag the body and put it on a gurney.

Marklin nodded.

The EMTs made quick work of the grim task while the CSIs kept close watch for more clues.

As the body bag was zipped shut, I glanced around and saw movement in the woods beyond the path.

A long-bearded man with wild, flowing grey hair emerged from between two bushes. He took one quick look at the cops and the death scene and immediately angled away. Despite the mid-summer heat, he appeared to be wearing at least two layers of grimy clothes. A heavy, ragged pack bounced slightly against his back as he pushed along with a sturdy, rough-hewn walking stick. He reminded me of photographs I had seen of swagmen, the Australian and New Zealand transients who carried and wore everything they owned while they hiked through the countryside searching for handouts and farm work.

Marklin and some of the uniformed cops briefly glanced up at the Swagman but stayed focused on other matters. One cop, however, detached himself from the death scene's periphery. He strode over and stopped the Swagman just as he reached the park's parking lot. The cop said something and pointed in our direction. The Swagman looked, said something and shook his head no.

The cop nodded. He gave the Swagman a friendly pat on the shoulder and let him go. As the cop returned to his post, he caught Marklin's attention and also shook his head no.

Marklin stuffed his small notebook into his shirt pocket, fastened its button and smiled at me. "Thanks for reviewing Dad's book," he said. "It was about the only review he got. Maybe you can write about his new novel once it's finished."

"Maybe so," I said.

I didn't tell him the book review editor received more than two hundred books a week for consideration and could, at most, print six or seven reviews.

We watched in respectful silence while the body was carried past us and past a small crowd of runners now jogging in place, anxious for the path to be opened again.

As soon as the yellow crime-scene tape was removed, Marklin waved the runners on their way. They surged off, some at a sedate pace, others sprinting and elbowing each other, competing to lead the pack.

Two runners immediately tripped over each other and fell, distracting a uniformed officer standing near the path. A runner right behind them suddenly veered toward us. He was tall and gangly, with very short, dark hair. He looked like someone who lived on a steady diet of wheatgrass and granola, with regular helpings of self-righteousness. His running attire, including shoes, probably had set him back at least a thousand bucks.

He jogged up to us and stopped. "Druggie, wetback or whore?" he said, nodding toward the spot where the woman had died.

Marklin said nothing. The runner looked at me. I shrugged.

The runner grinned smugly. "Either way, she got what she deserved."

4

Marklin glared at him. "Why's that?" He reached for his pen and notebook but stopped when he touched the button.

The runner smirked. "Just sayin'. Just sayin'."

He loped away and caught up with some of the other earnest runners moving along the jogging trail.

For a moment, I thought Marklin might chase after Mr. Granola and take him down with a flying tackle. But he let go of his pocket button and just watched him run. Now he looked at me.

"I'll tell Dad I met you."

"Tell him I said good luck with the new book."

We shook hands, and Marklin walked off toward the gathering of police vehicles.

Every bone and muscle ached when I reached the running trail's parking lot.

I climbed into my car and turned the key. After a while, it finally caught and chugged to life just as a few of the people in the parking lot turned to look.

I drove north on Lamar, thinking about Mr. Granola, the bullet hole and the woman's face.

I felt certain now about three things. Mr. Granola was a genuine jerk. I had seen the dead woman somewhere before. And, after ten years, I still liked reading and reviewing mystery novels.

Four things, actually.

I was certain I wanted nothing else to do with real murder investigations.

TWO

The next morning was pleasantly cool for mid-August, still in the low seventies at 9 a.m. The predicted high, however, was 105.

A slight breeze moved across my apartment balcony, bringing with it the lulling hums of air conditioners, lawnmowers and a distant Southwest 737.

I settled back in my white plastic balcony chair and opened the Sunday *Austin Daily Democrat*.

The Metro News section's "City Notes" column had a four-paragraph story about the woman. She was still unidentified. An unnamed police spokesman said that while her death appeared to be a homicide, suicide had not yet been ruled out. "A weapon has not been recovered, but someone could have found it and taken it," the spokesman said.

I tried again to remember where I had seen her. No clue.

I pulled out and opened the "Arts & Thought" section, ready to read my latest review.

I had penned some friendly touts of Marcus Darson's *The Mysterious Mister H*, the 28th novel in his best-selling Detective Jonahby series.

I had not read the whole paperback, of course, just sampled a few pages. But I had found a pithy quote and included it in my summation: *"Once again, gutsy Jonahby solves a dangerous case in spectacular fashion. With a Glock 9 blazing in each hand, he shouts 'Die, scumbags!'*

and saves his city, county and state the expense of a half-dozen murder trials. But does he also get the beautiful girl who hired him? You will have to read the book to find out."

There was a problem as I flipped through the "Arts & Thought" section. No book page. Somehow, the *ADD* had forgotten to print it. I turned back through the section and checked again. As a freelancer, I would get paid only *after* my review was published.

It wasn't there. Nobody's book review was there.

I called the book review editor, Robert Michaelsohn, at home.

"What?"

He sounded surly, hung over and still half asleep.

"The book page is missing," I said again.

"No, it's not," he said.

"Yes, it is. They forgot to print it."

"No, they didn't."

"Look in the paper. It's not there."

Robert coughed. I heard him light a cigarette, blow out some smoke and cough again. In the ten years I had known him, he had tried and failed to quit smoking at least fifteen times.

"It's not there," he said, "because it's gone."

"Gone?" How could a book review page be *gone*?

"Management shit-canned it yesterday to save money."

"You're kidding," I said.

"No, I'm not. The book page is history."

"Well, can you run my review somewhere else in the paper?" I sensed his answer even before he said it.

"No."

"Why not?"

"Ask me if I give a shit, Erwin."

It wasn't like Robert to talk this way.

"I *need* the one-fifty," I said. The *ADD* had been paying me $150 for each published review. I was counting on the money to supplement my monthly Social Security check.

"I need a *job*," Robert said. "They shit-canned me, too."

"Damn. *And* the reviewers?"

"You, especially," Robert said. "I was paying you twice as much as any of the other freelancers."

THREE

I drove to my favorite coffee bar, the Starbucks at 44th and Lamar, and sat at my favorite table. It was next to the north wall in a small alcove formed by a supporting column. The column helped keep the glare of the morning sun off my laptop computer's screen. And the table provided a fine view of the lined-up customers, the employees working the registers, and the condiments-and-napkins area where people added cream and sugar or diet creamers and artificial sweeteners after their drinks were announced.

"White chocolate mocha for Angie…on the bar! Skinny vanilla latte for Justin…on the bar! Caffe Americano for Brandon…on the bar!" Iced coffee with milk for Colleen…on the bar!"

Often, I peered over the top of my screen and admired the passing parade of women in nice business clothes, running shorts or tight jeans.

Today, however, as I drank an iced tea lemonade, I mostly just stared into space and wondered where else I might get paid to write book reviews.

The Starbucks was crowded with college students writing term papers or cramming for end-of-summer-semester tests. In the midst of them, a white-haired, white-bearded man in his early seventies was seated in a soft armchair. He quietly moved his lips and sipped from a small coffee as he read the *New York Times*.

At a table near the center of the store, however, one tall guy in his thirties apparently was trying hard to make everyone believe he was some kind of mobility mogul or telecommuting tycoon. He had two cell phones, one pressed to each ear, and a small videoconferencing microphone set up in front of his laptop.

He was, I suddenly realized, Mr. Granola, the wheatgrass- hole from the murder scene.

He pulled his microphone close to his mouth, muttered some words into it and then leaned closer to his computer screen.

The people at the other end of his flickering video link apparently were not hearing him well.

Mr. Granola grabbed the microphone and raised his voice. "Can you can hear me now?"

He said it loud enough that anyone inside the building could hear him. Eyes glanced at him. Heads bobbed up from computer screens, iPhones, newspapers and textbooks.

"I repeat, we won't actually *need* a product until we launch our brand and get some buzz going that creates demand!"

There was a garbled, barely audible response almost lost in the coffee shop's ambient noise.

"No, *need* – n-e-e-d – not seed!" Mr. Granola said.

All around him, people again looked up from their computers, newspapers, iPhones and textbooks, this time visibly irritated. Their glares had no effect.

Mr. Granola just gripped both cell phones tighter and pulled them to closer to his mouth. He didn't lower his voice.

"Mike! Tony! This videoconferencing link sucks! They can't hear me in Shanghai! Get me another link! *Link!* I said *link*, not *chink*!"

Even the people listening to their iPods with ear buds and headphones now looked around and stared at him.

The store's manager, a short, stocky guy with muscular forearms, came out from behind his counter and walked over to Mr. Granola, who was all but shouting into his microphone again.

"No! I repeat, *first* we build demand! *Then* we invest in product! No demand, no product!"

The manager leaned over, looked Mr. Granola directly in the eyes and said something quietly to him.

Visibly angry, Mr. Granola glared back at him. Then, deftly using his forearms, he scooped up his laptop and microphone without letting go of his cell phones. He stood up and bumped his chair with an elbow, so it fell over with a loud clatter.

"Mike!" he said into one of his cell phones. "They're throwing me out of Starbucks. Can you believe this friggin' shit?"

He stormed to the front door, pushed it open with his hip and strode out toward the parking lot, still yammering into his two cell phones as he kept his computer pressed to his chest with his elbows.

Many in the store applauded the manager. He acknowledged the plaudits with a slight nod and smile. He picked up the chair, wiped off the table and stepped back behind the counter.

Just as the atmosphere re-settled into Sunday morning calmness, my embarrassingly outdated candy bar cell phone suddenly rang.

The phone didn't play cool musical tones. It just made a loud, irritating ringing noise.

Nearby customers looked up at me and glared.

"Joan," the black-on-grey LCD screen dimly flashed.

I carried the phone outside and stood near the front door as it continued ringing and flashing: "Joan…Joan…Joan."

FOUR

Still visibly angry, Mr. Granola dumped his phones and computer into the passenger side of a black Porsche 911 Carrera GTS Coup. It was parked next to my dirty-blue 2002 Pontiac Sunfire.

M.G. strode around the front of his car and yanked open the driver's door. It hit my door hard enough to dent it, adding one more dent to the many parking-lot scars already there. He checked his door to see if it was damaged, visibly raged again and climbed in.

In two more rings, Joan's call would go to voice mail. I wasn't yet ready to tell her what I had just concluded: that, at age 63, I had *no* hope of landing new, paid work as a freelance book reviewer. By now, my few contacts at other newspapers were retired, dead or looking for new jobs, too.

Mr. Granola's Porsche roared out of the Starbucks parking lot as I pushed the green "Answer" button, and made a mental note of his personalized license plate – "MLTLVLMKG," multilevel marketing.

I would call my insurance company and report him, just in case he tried to claim I had damaged *his* car.

"Hello, sweetie," I said into my phone.

"I have this sick desire," Joan said, without preamble.

"For me?"

"For donuts and a Louis Vuitton bag," she said.

I grinned with relief. I wouldn't have to tell her my career fears. Not just yet.

"Is that what you want for your birthday?" I said. "A Louis Vuitton bag full of donuts?"

Joan, I realized, was being serious. She didn't laugh.

"I want them, Erwin, and I want them now. So here's the plan."

Joan Larson frequently had a plan. One of her favorite plans typically involved me strolling with her through malls and shopping centers, lugging an expanding burden of bags as we exited Nordstrom's, Macy's and several smaller, yet equally *tres chic*, retailers.

But she had many other facets to her personality. Sometimes, like a superbly cut diamond, she suddenly sparkled in unexpected ways. And those bright gleams often surprised, delighted – and sometimes irritated – me.

We had now been dating and spending most nights together for nearly five years.

By day, she was an on-the-go independent real-estate broker with a side penchant for donating modest amounts of money and time to causes that helped the ill, the homeless and the unemployed. She had grown up in Ames, Iowa, in a small family that operated a bundle-service laundry and coin-operated Laundromat barely a quarter mile from Iowa State University. Joan's first job, at age ten, had been folding shirts and pants. By high school, she was managing the Laundromat almost on her own, scooping out and counting the coins, handling the accounting and bank deposits and even doing minor repairs on the washers and dryers.

Her heart, however, was on being actress. She had tried being in some of Ames High School's plays and musicals. But having a business to take care of before and after school meant she had no time to rehearse for starring roles.

The best she had been able to do was sing and dance in the chorus for *Oklahoma!* and help get costumes altered and cleaned for *Arsenic and Old Lace.*

Once she turned eighteen and graduated from high school, her parents wanted her to remain in Ames, enroll at State, and take a bigger role in the family laundry empire. But Joan had her heart and her young life savings set on majoring in theater at the University of Texas at Austin.

Since age thirteen, she had very carefully saved most of her earnings, as well as orphan coins – the ones that rolled under washers and dryers or jammed in coin slots or were agitated out of pants and left behind by customers.

At UT, Joan had landed plenty of minor and major roles in plays, musicals, operas and student films. But her Iowa Laundromat seed money quickly had run out, so she had taken a part-time office job in one of Austin's largest real estate brokerage firms, intending to remain a lowly office clerk who just answered phones, set appointments and filed papers while she paid for college and performed. By the time she graduated, however, her degree was in business administration, with a minor in theater, and she also had earned a Texas real estate broker's license and was leasing commercial properties and selling houses.

Ironically, she had made the switch to business late in her sophomore year, while helping with costumes and lighting for *Death of a Salesman.* In her epiphany, she had realized that a theatrical career likely would leave her always grubbing for coins, just as she had done back in Ames. Meanwhile, God wasn't making any more land, as her grandfatherly boss at the real estate office liked to point out. And the world's buildings and houses could be looked upon as a massive stage that bore a cast of billions in constantly changing human drama with trillions of dollars at stake.

And real estate agents always had to act and appear prosperous even when they weren't.

Changing from theater to business would *not* be a waste of an expensive, hard-earned education, Joan wisely had decided. Just a redirection of her talents.

"You're taking me," Joan said now in my phone, "to Mrs. Johnson's Donuts over on Airport Boulevard. And then we're going to the Louis Vuitton store at The Domain."

"Are you asking me for a date?"

I liked to tweak the tigress's tail, sometimes.

"If you truly love me, Erwin Tennyson, you will be here in thirty minutes."

"Then what happens, after we've eaten the donuts from the five-hundred-dollar bag?"

"Thirteen," she said. "Thirteen hundred."

"A *thirteen*-hundred-dollar handbag?"

"I sold a house today. Million five."

"Wow, at six percent – "

"*Don't* do the math," she said. "You'll get depressed."

She was right. I was living on Social Security and an early-retirement pension that generously could be described as pitiful.

"Okay. What happens after we eat the donuts and I'm completely mesmerized by the bag?" I said.

"Well, we haven't made love in three days," she said.

"I can do *that* math."

"Thirty minutes, Erwin."

For a sixty-year-old, Joan Larson still looked hot, hot, hot. And I had a fresh, prescription bottle of what my doctor grinningly referred to as "plumbing helper."

The time *after* shopping was shaping up very nicely.

"I'll be there in fifteen," I said. "And the donuts are on me."

"But not the bag."

"In my next life, maybe."

"It's okay, Erwin," Joan said, her voice sparkling now. "I love you for your mind and your cute little butt, not your bank account."

Lucky me, I thought, as we hung up and I sucked down the last, icy drops of my drink. *Lucky, lucky me.*

FIVE

My Sunfire lived up to its name when I climbed into it. It had been baking in the August sun for two hours while I luxuriated at Starbucks. Now its black seats were scalding and I barely could touch its steering wheel without burning my hands. Fortunately, it started up nicely, on the third try.

I pulled out onto Lamar and deftly dodged a sudden lane change by a speeding, pearl-colored BMW sedan.

The Beamer had four big dogs and a bundle of party balloons inside.

It may have had a driver, too. I couldn't be sure.

In Austin, Texas, the world capital of weird, you never could be *sure* about anything.

I headed north, grateful that my car was paid for and still running after 164,327 miles.

An hour later, Joan lovingly clutched her new Louis Vuitton handbag. And I still had tasty traces of donut sugar around my mouth.

Now we were on the west side of Austin, in Barton Creek Square Mall, taking a side trip to find some Jimmy Choos.

I had been ready to go straight to Joan's house after the Louis-and-donuts expedition. She knew how much I hated driving Highway 2222, or any Austin road, at rush hour. But she also wanted new heels to match her new bag.

"Maybe I'll wear the Jimmy Choos while we make love," she said.

I voiced no more complaints about the traffic. I even stayed patient at the wheel while we searched for and finally found a parking space just a short walk from the retail boutique that carried the lust-worthy shoes.

"See, that wasn't so bad," Joan said with a mischievous grin. She patted my backside as we walked out into the mall's central corridor. I carried her new $400 package, while she held onto the Louis Vuitton and protected it like a football.

We made one more stop, at an upscale toy retailer, so I could help her pick out a birthday gift for the youngest of her four grandsons.

"I have a much easier time shopping for little girls than little boys," Joan said as she looked over the big array of toy robots, laser guns, space battle cruisers and monster trucks.

I picked up a battery-powered monster truck, one that featured laser machine guns, flashing police lights and a piercing, multi-tone siren.

"He'll like this," I said.

Joan looked at it, dubious.

"Trust me," I said. "I wish I had one, too."

Joan smirked as she paid for it and had it gift-wrapped. "If he or his mother hates it," she said, "you'll be getting it for Christmas."

"Cool!"

When we left the toy store, I led her across the corridor to a frozen-yogurt shop. I bought us each a small cone of chocolate-vanilla swirl. *Last of the big spenders.*

"It's not a diamond ring," I said as I bowed slightly and presented her treat. "But it's still a symbol of my love."

Joan smiled, took a small bite and got a faraway look. "If we were married, they'd be your grandkids, too."

"But we're not."

"And we don't want to be."

"That's right."

"Why mess up a perfectly good relationship by making it boringly legal. Anyway," Joan added, between two more bites, "you've been married several times already."

We started walking.

"Just twice. One time fewer than you," I said.

My most recent marriage had ended seven years ago, when my then fifty-year-old wife decided to move to West Hollywood, California, with a lesbian lover who was half my age. Her aerobics salsa instructor.

Joan's third marriage also had ended seven years ago, when her husband suddenly announced he was gay and moved to Bangor, Maine, to live with a man he had met on Facebook.

Joan and I had that in common: the shock of sudden spousal orientation changes. And she had been the real estate agent who listed and eventually sold my house after my divorce was granted.

That was how we met – and why we quickly ended up sleeping with each other. We both needed to know we were *okay*.

We were.

Now, half a decade later, we were more than okay. We were *torrid*, at least twice a week.

Three things happened suddenly as we continued walking and eating our frozen yogurts:

An alarm sounded and lights flashed at the front of a nearby music and video store.

Two, a young man in his early twenties raced out the store's entrance and sprinted toward us. He was looking back at:

Three, a pair of mall cops, one short and one tall. Mutt and Jeff were giving chase.

Suddenly, they all ran straight at us, and a collision appeared imminent. My first instinct was to protect Joan and her Louis Vuitton from the impact. But there was no time.

I put my head down, charged forward two quick steps and tackled the shoplifter low, near the ankles, exactly the way I had been taught on the 1965 Claudius Morton Junior High School football "B" team.

Coach What's-His-Name Pepper would have been proud. Maybe even a bit sorry he had left me sitting on the bench almost all season.

The frozen-yogurt cone and the Jimmy Choos bag both crunched into the backs of the guy's legs as we hit the tile. He was wearing faded jeans, well-worn New Balance shoes – an orange "N" logo was right in my face now – and a flannel shirt over a grey T-shirt, even though it was summer.

The mall cops grabbed him and had him up and cuffed in seconds.

"Get the LP detectives here A-SAP!" I heard Mall Cop Mutt say into his radio.

What's an LP detective? I wondered as I struggled to my knees, leaving frozen yogurt handprints on the tile.

For a moment, I thought I heard a cheering crowd. *Tennyson scores!*

Then I heard Joan say frantically: "Erwin! Are you okay? Are you hurt?"

Mall Cop Jeff put in his tall two cents. "You okay, man?"

The cheering crowd quickly degenerated into a high-pitched whine. I realized I had caught a knee to my forehead and gotten my bell rung.

"I'm okay," I said, still on my knees. The high-pitched whine faded, and I felt a slight rush of testosterone as Joan gently pulled the Jimmy Choos bag from my sticky hand. *That was Tennyson on the tackle for a loss of ten yards!*

I didn't try to stand up yet. Deep inside an unseen tunnel, cheerleaders were still chanting. *"Erwin, Erwin, he's our man! If he can't do it, no one can!"*

"I didn't mean to!" I heard the shoplifter say. My head cleared as I looked up.

A muscular man in his early thirties and a young woman in her twenties hurried over from the music and video store. The young woman's tastefully stylish sales clothes did not quite hide the tattoos of dragons, skulls and knives on her forearms.

The muscular guy reached into the shoplifter's flannel shirt and pulled out a CD.

"Dude, you're going down!" Muscles said, waving the CD in the shoplifter's face. "We got you with the goods." It was something by Lady Gaga. Or Cher. I didn't get a good look.

"I've never done this before!" the young man protested as Muscles and the Tattooed Lady marched him back toward the store. "I was trying to get my girlfriend a birthday gift! I don't have a job! I don't have any money! Please let me go!"

I felt bad for him yet pleased with my prowess as I gradually stood up and made sure I could remain vertical.

Joan clutched her bags with one hand and squeezed my arm with the other. "Are you sure you're okay?"

I nodded. In all my years reviewing crime fiction, I had never heard of LP detectives.

I gestured toward Muscles and the Tattooed Lady. "What do they do?" I said to Mall Cop Mutt.

"What you just did, man," Mutt said with a grin. "Loss prevention. They stop shoplifters."

Mentally, I made the connection between "LP" and "loss prevention," but the only image that still came clearly to mind was a black vinyl disc with a red label, turning at 33-1/3 rpm on a record player.

Right now, I just wanted to lie down on Joan's big bed and watch her strut around with nothing on but the new Jimmy Choos and her Louis Vuitton handbag.

First, however, there was an award ceremony.

The music and video store's manager hurried into the corridor, thanked me and handed me a gift card "good for ten percent off anything we sell."

As I looked at the card, two city cops hustled in to take the shoplifter to jail.

I figured the store had nothing in stock by Michael Praetorius, Domenico Scarlatti, Georg Philipp Telemann, or any of the other stars of the 16th, 17th and 18th centuries.

You can't head-bang to Baroque; you can't reggae to Renaissance. Yet, for Joan and me, those and 13th century choral music were the perfect genres for making love.

I handed the discount card to a passing teenager as Joan and I headed toward the exit.

I took one of her bags, held her hand and grinned as once again I heard, very faintly, somewhere deep within my rattled head: *Tennyson scores!*

SIX

I waited until afterward to tell Joan that my freelance book review gig was gone.

"I may have to get a part-time job," I said.

I hoped she wouldn't be too shocked or disappointed.

"Good," she said. She opened her shoe closet and added the Jimmy Choos to her extensive collection. "You'll like having more money to spend." The unspoken subtext, of course, was: "*And so will I.*"

Her shoes were well-arranged by brand. The new heels went into the "C," not "J," section, I noted.

Joan shut the closet's accordion doors, eased into her king-sized bed and stretched out beside me. "Anyway, you've said you were tired of doing dust-jacket journalism."

When we first started dating two years ago, she had asked how I could review books I barely had time to read before deadline.

Easy, I said.

I found most information for a review right on a hardback's dust jacket. It was in the story summary that also served as the book's sales pitch. Then I read the "About the Author" paragraph and scanned the overly done praises by well-known authors who likely had not read the book, either.

"I just rewrite some of that and add a stock reviewer's phrase or two, such as 'enticing, engrossing crime fiction' or "nonstop twists and thrills.""

"Dust-jacket journalism," she had said dismissively.

She rolled over now and gave me a kiss. "So what's your new career choice?"

"I'm thinking," I said.

"You have no idea."

She was absolutely correct.

For the past thirty years, I had worked only for newspapers, starting out as a general-assignments reporter and eventually moving up to feature writer. In my final decade, all at the *Austin Daily Democrat*, I had just written short reviews of books the unwashed public happily consumed. These were the works the newspaper's "literary" critics deemed well beneath their dignity to review: Westerns, World War II novels, spy tales, science fiction tomes, two-fisted mysteries. Lately, I had been reviewing more and more detective novels.

But it wasn't all dust-jacket journalism. Paperback novels, after all, had no dust jackets. And their smaller covers provided less room for information I could…borrow.

So I always flipped through a few pages and made damned sure the paperback's author could write coherent sentences before I declared: *"…a brilliant debut thriller by an outstanding new Texas writer."*

None of that mattered now. Newspapers everywhere were eliminating book reviews and sacking their book reviewers.

I was been luckier than most. Just before the Great Recession dropped toward its nadir, I had cobbled together what had seemed a fine early retirement plan: a monthly Social Security check supplemented with freelance book reviews for my ex-employer. I had even been given a brief retirement party in a *Daily Democrat* conference room: coconut cake, a small bowl of fruit punch and a funny going-away card signed by some of the newsies and photographers.

Robert Michaelsohn and the other staff reviewers, however, had gotten their belongings handed to them in cardboard boxes. Then the *Daily Democrat* security guards escorted them out to their cars and carefully scraped off their employee parking stickers before they were allowed to leave.

I never imagined the *Daily Democrat* would fight shrinking circulation and rising printing costs by axing book reviews. To me, those had been the newspaper's creative heartbeat. Unlike the hard-charging investigative reporters who had to dig through turgid documents and browbeat reluctant sources, we reviewers got to sit on our butts in our cubicles and sagely just make things up.

What, indeed, would I do next?

I wondered about this even after Joan returned to bed, snuggled close to me and quickly fell asleep. Aside from typing, writing short book reviews was my only verifiable job skill.

Would I have to take classes? Get a Microsoft mumbo-jumbo certification? Learn to create Excel spreadsheets and PowerPoint presentations?

Depicting *what*?

I had no desire to go back to school and be the Almost Oldest Man on Campus.

Why couldn't I just go to the nearest convenience store and pick up a winning Mega-Billions lottery ticket?

Some people have all the luck.

No, they don't, I thought the next morning as I woke just before dawn and felt Joan's smooth warmth against my back.

They absolutely do not *have* all *the luck.*

SEVEN

Joan's first appointment of the day was to show an $800,000 house, a ranch-style stone "fixer-upper" perched high atop a cedar-covered hill about five miles west of Highway 620.

"And then I have a wah-wah luncheon," she said.

"Wah-wah?"

"West Austin Women's Advocates. We help find and support safe housing for battered women."

"Sounds kind of earnest and grim – the luncheon," I said.

"Actually, we wear silly hats, sing the wah-wah fight song and write checks to support women's shelters. Then we eat lunch and gossip for thirty minutes about husbands and boyfriends."

"Do you gossip about me?" I said.

"Not much," Joan said. "I just say you're smart and sexy and superb in the sack. And my smile says the rest. You *are*, you know."

She gave me a kiss and left.

I stood around for moment feeling smart, sexy and superb. Then I took a shower and tried to figure out how I would spend the rest of my day. In the midst of shampooing my thinning hair, I suddenly remembered where I had seen the dead woman in the park while she was still alive.

Not at a WAWA luncheon.

Three weeks ago, I had gone to "Deep in the Heart of Texas Novels," a low-budget reception put on by a locally-owned Austin bookstore that was struggling to keep its doors open in the recession. Seven local authors were supposed to appear, make some brief remarks, shake a few hands and autograph any copies of their books purchased that evening for ten percent off.

Three of the authors, however, were on tight schedules, flying back to Austin from other cities. Their planes had been grounded or diverted by severe thunderstorms over Tennessee and North Texas.

When one of the bookstore employees announced to the crowd – in English and Spanish – that Jan Reid, David Lindsey and Frank Arkandale had all telephoned their regrets and promised to appear some other night, the young woman immediately had wadded up her event brochure, thrown it and her empty plastic wine glass to the floor. Then, muttering something I could not hear, she had left the store empty-handed and visibly angry. She had appeared to be a very emotional fan of one of the three writers.

After I dried off and pulled on my underwear, I located Sgt. Marklin's card in my wallet and gave him the basic details in a voice message. Then I dressed for the day: blue jeans, tan polo shirt and running shoes that had not yet run a single stride.

He called me back while I was climbing into my car, trying to decide whether my first morning snack would be a Mrs. Johnson's donut or a Torchy's breakfast taco.

"Thanks. It's a starting point, Mister Tennyson," he said. "Do you happen to know if they took reservations or had some kind of guest list?"

"It was open to the public," I said. "I think about fifty people were there. I didn't see anyone I knew."

I heard the value of my clue diminishing quickly as Sgt. Marklin said "Hmm."

"Well, I'll take her picture out to the bookstore soon. Maybe one of the employees will recognize her."

"PhotoShopped?" I said.

I knew I wouldn't want to look at any gruesome pictures of what I had already seen. I hoped he would do something to hide the hideous gunshot wound.

He knew exactly what I meant.

"Oh, absolutely," he said. "We'll edit out the bullet hole and paste in some open eyes. She'll appear somewhat alive in the headshot."

We ended the call, and I started my Sunfire's aging engine. It came to life on the second try.

As I drove away from Joan's house, I still couldn't decide: *Breakfast donut or breakfast taco?* My dashboard clock flashed straight-up 11:00 a.m.

I made up my mind: *Lunch!*

EIGHT

I had a chicken gyro sandwich at a little Greek deli on Hancock Road. Then, from my umbrella-shaded table, I sipped the last of my diet Coke and called Robert Michaelsohn to see if he had found a new job. I hoped, of course, it would be one that offered gigs for freelance book reviewers.

"Nope. I've made a hundred phone calls and sent out three hundred resumes. There doesn't seem to be a job market for unemployed book page editors."

"What are you going to do?"

"I've got some possibilities," he said. "My stepbrother has a fishing boat in Alaska. He lost one of his crewmen in the Bering Sea last week."

I had read a detective novel once that involved Arctic fishermen and some *very* cold-blooded murders. "That's one of the worst places on Earth," I said. "He'd let you *do* that?"

"Sure. We didn't get along all that well when we were kids."

After we hung up, I drove back to my apartment. I took my computer out onto my balcony, sat in my white plastic chair and stared at the barrier of trees. The day was alive with August heat and the sounds of distant sirens, commerce, neighborhood dogs and birds.

Robert Michaelsohn was my last link for staying inside the floundering newspaper business. If his best and brightest hope was a job on an Alaskan fishing boat, I was well and truly screwed.

I got online and surfed for a miracle.

There were none. But Sgt. Marklin's father had sent me an email. He wanted to buy me a coffee and tell me about his new novel.

I replied that I hated coffee, but I'd happily settle for an iced tea lemonade.

When I met him early the next morning at my favorite Starbucks, I recognized him right away. In the face, at least, he looked like an older edition of his son. He came straight to my table.

"Ranger Marklin," I said.

"Call me Big Paul," he said. He shook my hand.

Big Paul did not exactly live up to his nickname. He was thin and wiry and might have stood 5-9 in Texas Ranger cowboy boots. But in brown sandals, tan cargo shorts and a red-and-yellow Hawaiian shirt, he looked more like a vacationing proctologist or finance professor than a recently retired state cop.

He got himself a black coffee and brought me an iced tea lemonade refill.

After he sat down, we made preliminary small talk about the August heat. He got a text message on his cell phone.

He grinned as he read it. "Little Paul says he's gonna stop by for a minute."

"Little Paul?"

Little Paul – Sgt. Marklin – towered over both of us when he stood at our table holding his morning mocha.

"My brothers were tall. I was the runt," Big Paul said.

"You still are," Little Paul said, smiling as he rubbed the top of his father's bald head.

"But I can still eat you under the table. And..."

Big Paul suddenly stood up and – in a flash – grabbed Little Paul's left wrist, twisted it, and had it behind the young cop's back.

"Ow, Dad!" Little Paul said. He tried to turn out of Big Paul's grip. He also tried to not spill his mocha.

"I can still beat your ass," Big Paul said, grinning as he let go.

Little Paul rubbed his wrist against one leg and winced as he took a mocha sip. "You're the man," he said.

"Damn straight I'm the man," Big Paul said proudly. "Except I'm retired and now *you're* the man. Remember that move, son."

Little Paul took another taste of his drink. "I will, Dad. I'll use it the next time I bust somebody who's holding a mocha in a coffee shop."

"What do you call that maneuver?" I said to Big Paul as he sat down again.

He smirked. "The triple expresso take-down."

"Really."

"He's bullshittin' you," Little Paul said. He rubbed his wrist against his pants leg again.

"I *am* bullshittin' you," Big Paul said to me. "Most good cops can make that move after a double expresso. But the really good cops, like me, can pull it off after consuming just one hot chocolate or diet Coke."

"He's full of it, and he stays full of it," Little Paul said, smirking. "I'm off to work."

"I love you, too, son." Big Paul didn't hide his pride as Little Paul started to leave.

"Anything new on the park case?" I said.

Sgt. Marklin stopped and looked back at me. "Which park case? I'm working a dozen park cases."

"The one on Lamar. The jogging trail."

The detective looked over my head for a moment, his eyes focused on nothing visible. He seemed to be mentally flipping through file folders. "The Jane Doe," he said finally. "Not a thing."

He left. Big Paul got himself a black coffee and bought me an iced tea lemonade refill. The Starbucks was crowded now with stylishly dressed young women and young men in suits and business-casual clothes. Most were standing in line or waiting for drinks, visibly anxious to head off for their jobs.

"Actually, I'm not quite ready to talk about my book," Big Paul said. He stirred in two sugar packets. "I just want to know the best ways to get it reviewed once it's published."

I took a long sip of my drink and then I told him the truth, how newspapers were cutting back or completely eliminating book reviews, how I had just lost my freelance gig and how I no longer had any juice anywhere on the planet as a reviewer.

"I was afraid of that," he said quietly. "Some of my other contacts say it's tough out there and getting tougher. Well, could you maybe help me get a review in the *American-Statesman*?"

Since I had worked at the *Daily Democrat*, I probably could not even get my own obituary into the *Statesman*, its chief competitor. I told him that. "But I'll try."

He nodded and looked disappointed. "Well, maybe I'll need an editor," he said.

I hated, loathed, *detested* editing book manuscripts. But I didn't tell him that.

In the back of my mind, I could hear my poor mother lecturing me eons ago. *"Erwin,"* she used to say, *"beggars who try to be choosers will always end up losers."* As a young girl, she and her family had almost starved to death during the Great Depression. Piece by piece, they had sold off everything they owned. Then one night they gathered around their last possession, an old upright piano, in their empty, rented house and sang a few final hymns. "Will the Circle Be Unbroken?" was the last. The next morning, they sold the piano, too. Then one of Mother's uncles came by in a truck that barely ran and carried the family out to his beaten-down farm a few miles outside of town.

For the next two years, Mother and her family lived in the uncle's drafty barn. They didn't want to do farming. But they did want to eat. So they planted, grew and consumed almost any kind of food that would sprout.

When nothing else was available, they harvested wild dandelion greens and boiled them into a bitter winter soup that they could flavor with a precious teaspoon of lard and sometimes a small, overlooked onion still in the ground after the fall harvest. Mother's moral was always the same: *"Be grateful for what you have and take any opportunity for honest work."*

"I might be available to do some editing work," I told Big Paul. I took a long pull of iced tea lemonade. "Do you miss being a Ranger?"

He grinned. "All those crooks, dead people and corrupt politicians? Oh, hell, no. I *never* liked being a Ranger. Long hours. Lousy pay. God-awful assignments. But it paid better than being a deputy sheriff in Cottle County. It was a steady job with state benefits, and I had a family to support. So I just did what I had to do."

"Lot of that going around," I said, gesturing at the younger people crowded at the tables around us. They all appeared to be uploading resumes, trying to make online sales, or struggling to finish degrees in business, marketing or law.

Big Paul saw what I saw and nodded. "Yep." He took a sip of his coffee and studied his cup for a moment. "I'd say we retired just in time."

NINE

A few hours after we left Starbucks, I emailed Big Paul. I asked him how I could trace a license plate. I told him briefly how somebody driving a Porsche with "MLTLVLMK" plates had damaged my passenger-side door and left the scene of the "accident."

I didn't say "Mr. Granola," and I didn't mention the dozen or so other dents in my Sunfire.

I figured if Mr. Granola filed a damage claim and drove up my insurance rates, I might motor over to his address some stormy night and accidentally stomp a big dent into his Porsche's passenger-side door.

Vengeance is mine!

That evening, Big Paul sent me a response. "You can't trace it. Not legally. You'll need to file a police report. Hypothetically speaking, however, if someone did trace it, the computer screen might display a name and address in the following format."

The name he listed, "Garpmann Rich," definitely looked hypothetical. The address, however, was real: a high-dollar apartment complex overlooking Capitol of Texas Highway in West Austin.

I had been there once with Joan. One of her real-estate friends, an apartment locator, had been rushed to the hospital to have a baby two weeks early, and Joan had volunteered to handle the young woman's showings without sharing any of her commissions. Joan also had rounded up and delivered a handsome collection of baby-shower gifts from the young woman's friends. Her husband was a supply sergeant somewhere in Afghanistan, and her parents were somewhere in Montana, out of cell phone range, moseying toward Texas in their retirement RV, unaware that their grandson had been born early. The complex, I recalled, had a nice view of downtown Austin to the east about eight miles away and, to the west, you could see the rolling Texas Hill Country. Leases, Joan had told me, went for somewhere between $1,850 and $3,000 a month. You didn't work at Whataburger and live there.

I glanced at the hypothetical vehicle listed in Big Paul's message. It was a brown 1962 Corvair four-door sedan.

I laughed. No one with any semblance of a right mind would put personalized "Multi-level Marketing" plates on a car deemed "unsafe at any speed" nearly 50 years ago. But Big Paul also had no reason to give me an example name and address. Maybe I was getting more help than I initially thought.

I Googled "Garpmann Rich" and came up with multiple links, including "Rich Garpmann, multi-level marketing consultant" and "Rich Garpmann, Mister Multi-level Marketing in Austin." The latter website included a headline: "Learn MLM from the Best!" It also had a picture of Garpmann standing next to his washed-and-polished Porsche. In his hands, just beneath his greedy grin, he was holding $100 bills fanned out like cards. Nearly $3,000 by my count.

A kick to his car door likely would add up to just a minor business tax deduction.

There was one other noteworthy link. A news release had been posted last month by an Austin public relations agency: "Marketing Consultant Elected President of West Austin Pistol & Rifle Club."

The release noted that Garpmann recently had won his third classic pistol-shooting competition in a row, using his "favorite" .38-caliber Walther PPK, "which his grandfather liberated from a Nazi S.S. officer during World War II." The release further noted that the acronym "PPK" stood for "Polizeipistole Kriminellmodell (police pistol, detective model)."

Maybe I would *not* kick his car.

Maybe I would just send some evil vibes his way and hope that someone else, or something, perhaps a tire-catapulted rock, would ding his door.

But why, I wondered, did "Kriminellmodell" *not* mean "criminal model"? Was a German detective actually called a "kriminell"? Did the gun maker actually sell a "criminal model" of its pistol?

I did some quick Web searches.

"Kriminell," indeed, was the German word for "criminal."

And "detektiv" was a German word for "detective."

But on the third try, I discovered that "kriminal" also was a German word for "detective." A German detective novel was known as a "kriminalroman."

The PR agency's news release contained an unfortunate typo. And so, I discovered, did several gun websites popular with Walther PKK owners.

I felt like a master "kriminal" as I shut down my laptop computer for the night.

TEN

The next morning, I woke up trying to remember a particular line from a Sherlock Holmes short story I had once read. I had no idea why.

Joan stirred as I climbed out of bed. I promised I would wake her in 15 minutes.

"Thirty would be better," she said. She was asleep again in seconds.

In her spacious kitchen, I watched her digital coffeepot turn itself on and begin its burbling magic. I liked the smell of fresh coffee as it brewed. And I hated its nasty, bitter, vile taste each time I tried to drink it.

I put some ice in a glass, poured in a few ounces of Diet Coke and felt some bubbles tickle my nose as I drank it. It would have to sustain me until I could wrap my hand around an iced tea lemonade later in the morning.

Joan was not a great fan of mystery stories, yet she kept a few detective tales on one of her bookshelves in her well-decorated and efficient home office off the kitchen: three P.D. James paperbacks, two well-worn Dorothy Sayers novels and two crisp collections of Sherlock Holmes short stories by Sir Arthur Conan Doyle. I had read them all.

I opened one of the short story collections, thumbed through it, and finally found the quote I was seeking. Two pages into "The Boscombe Valley Mystery," Sherlock tells his faithful sidekick, Dr. John Watson: "The more featureless and commonplace a crime is, the more difficult it is to bring it home."

I had no idea why this had floated up in the middle of a vague waking dream.

Had the young woman's death in the park triggered it? Was it a "featureless and commonplace" crime? Or was it simply suicide? If so, what had driven her to it?

Did Mr. Granola – smug Mr. MLTLVLMKT Asshole – somehow fit into her death?

I hated waking up this way. I took another diet Coke wakeup chug. Then I sat down at Joan's computer and checked my email accounts. The only new message of consequence was from "Barrister Paul Nkomba" in Lagos, Nigeria, informing me that my long-lost unnamed cousin, who apparently had been that country's "esteemed" vice air minister, had just died and left me "150$ Million USD." All I had to do was send Barrister Nkomba my name, address, Social Security number, credit card number, credit card password and complete bank information. The "150$ Million USD" then would be wired directly to my checking account in minutes, I was promised.

I replied posthaste to the dear barrister: "Please use the money to create jobs in Nigeria. Build a 1,500-foot-tall monument to my dear cousin and keep the change."

Joan still had 18 minutes to snooze. So I Googled some course catalogs for Austin's universities.

The prices shocked me. A single three-semester-hour class now cost more than I had spent on a full academic load in the Sixties. Just one semester of my new, as-yet-unknown career path would cost almost all of a year's Social Security payments.

Forty years ago, I had borrowed four hundred bucks to finish my final semester of journalism school. It would be absurd now to borrow fifty, sixty or even seventy thousand dollars for a new four-year degree. I would be 67, pushing 68, when I graduated.

Who would hire an entry-level accountant, librarian or marketing specialist who also happened to be a doddering senior citizen?

I could go to a much-cheaper community college and, for just a few thousand dollars, get a two-year certificate in auto body repair, dental hygiene or astronomy. But I would be 65, pushing 66, the day I hit the job market, ready to sand, scrape or stare.

Bottom line, I couldn't afford the student loans, I was running out of lifetime, and none of the degree programs sounded remotely interesting. It was the perfect storm in which to start a new, post-retirement career.

I closed Joan's browser, padded back to the bedroom and kissed her awake for another day of trying to sell million-dollar houses and trying to help the misfortunate.

"Five more minutes," she said. She pulled the sheet and bedspread up to the top of her head.

She would, I knew, offer to help me go back to school if I brought it up. But we also had made a deal two years ago when we started dating, both of us fresh from painful, costly divorces: I would keep my own roof over my head, drive my own car, not spend beyond my means, and sometimes take us out for Thai food, hamburgers, gelato or a movie. And I would not let a certain expensive prescription run out.

I had no problem with that. Sometimes, I didn't even need the plumbing help. Joan was that good.

I crawled into bed with her. Momentarily, I wondered if I should have driven a harder bargain with Barrister Paul Nkomba. I could have offered to take over the vice air minister's post for a modest fee and strut around Austin in a uniform resplendent with epaulets, medals and braid.

The murder scene, however, floated into my mind again: Sgt. Marklin, Mr. Granola, the Swagman, the uniformed cops – and the dozens of runners seemingly unconcerned about anything except their strides, their digitally measured heart rates and their well-appointed combinations of logo clothing.

I couldn't stop thinking about all that the young woman would never know or have again.

Hopes. Dreams. Desires. Career.

Love. Marriage. Children.

I snuggled up against Joan, wrapped my arms around her and held on for dear life.

ELEVEN

Robert Michaelsohn called that evening. He sounded happy and upbeat. He had, he said, found a "challenging and exciting" new job. Coming from him, these were odd words.

A local investor, he explained, was launching an arts and entertainment website and wanted to include a few reviews of books written by Texas authors.

"I thought of you right away," Robert said.

"How much will it pay?"

"Are you sitting down?"

I was standing at my kitchen counter, ready to microwave some chicken noodle soup. Joan had two showings today, both during the lunch hour, so I was on my own as a magic chef.

I set the timer to one minute and pushed the "Start" button. Intense microwave radio beams immediately and violently assaulted the little bits of chicken and the salty broth molecules.

"I'm sitting now," I said. Actually, I was just leaning over the counter. But now I had a reporter's notebook open and a ballpoint pen at the ready.

"Your earning potential is unlimited," Robert said.

His voice had a particular tone I had heard from car salesmen and time-share hucksters but never from newspaper journalists.

"What does that mean in round dollars?"

"The more advertising we sell," Robert said, "the more we will make. We'll get a percentage of every ad."

"How much will you *pay* me for each review?"

"Your earning potential is unlimited," Robert repeated.

I looked at the marks I had made on my notepad. They added up to exactly nothing.

I began to understand what he was saying. "You're going to pay me nothing? *Free* reviews?"

"No, Erwin, I *explained* it," Robert said. "We'll get a percentage of every ad we sell. A *nice* percentage."

"What do you mean 'we sell'? Who will be selling the advertising?"

"You and me. We'll get bookstores and bars and coffeehouses to advertise on our web page, and we'll split thirty percent of every ad we sell."

"We're newsies. We don't sell ads," I said.

"In the brave new world of new media, yes we do," Robert said. "I've got space for six reviews this week. You can write them all, and we can team up and ride together when we go out to do the ad sales."

I couldn't believe it. Robert Michaelsohn had been unemployed for less than a month and already he had gone over to journalism's darkest side.

I wanted to tell him no and throw my cell phone against the nearest wall. But beneath my disgust, I realized what was happening.

He was a long way from retirement, and he had nothing else going on.

The odd undertone in Robert Michaelsohn's voice, I suddenly knew, was fear. He was scared to death.

"Let me think about it," I said.

"Let me know by tomorrow. The investor is eager to launch," Robert said.

I hung up thinking *Launch?Launch?*

Already I missed "*Roll the presses!*"

TWELVE

At 7 a.m. the next morning, my favorite table was available, and someone had left behind a wrinkled "Business Day" section from the *New York Times*. I also had a customer-loyalty coupon good for a free drink. It was my lucky day at Starbucks.

Now if I could just find a job that *paid*.

My laptop marched through its long, slow boot-up while I sucked down some of the iced tea lemonade's cold, sharp sweetness and scanned the *Times* headlines:

"Tax Increase Would Not Hurt Small Business" … "S.E.C. Wants Debt Rule Reinstated"… "Chinese Conglomerate Makes Bid for MGM" … "Tech Firm Cited for Recruiting Scam" … "Consumer Prices Remain Steady."

Gmail came up, and I checked for responses to the resume I had posted yesterday on Monster.com, in the crowded "journalists seeking jobs" category.

Zip. Nada. Zero.

Barrister Paul Nkomba was back, however, with more sad-but-good news from Lagos. Now, a long-lost, unnamed uncle, a former vice president of Nigeria, had died suddenly and left me "250$ billion USD." And it was ready for immediate transfer to my bank account if I would just blah, blah, blah. I replied to the good barrister telling him he should buy himself a business-class ticket to hell. "But do keep the change," I added helpfully.

By 7:15 a.m., the going-to-work crowd was lined up almost out the door. Employees were taking orders at both cash registers, and behind them, three baristas were doing their bump-and-twist drink dance and calling out the lattes, mochas, frappuccinos, smoothies, coffees and teas that were now on the bar.

Sgt. Marklin walked in and joined the line. He was dressed in tan pants, a white short-sleeved shirt, and dark-brown walking shoes. He yawned as he stared at the menu board and adjusted his gun belt. I recognized his pistol. A Glock, likely a Model 23. Out of curiosity, I had Googled "popular police guns" while writing my now-unpublished Detective Jonahby review.

Marklin's belt also had silver handcuffs, a cell phone, and a pouch for spare clips. And his shield was pinned to it. He poured a little cream and a lot of sugar into his mocha and came right toward me as he was leaving.

"How's it going?" I said.

He stopped at my table and took a sip. "Still no ID. Chief said we'll file it as a Jane Doe suicide unless we get more info."

"What about UT and the other schools?"

"Been there, done that. No one's missing."

"Did you find any footprints?"

Marklin laughed. "Along a running trail? We'd have footprints by the thousands."

"Sorry," I said, feeling embarrassed. "Just trying to be helpful."

He nodded and took another sip of his coffee. "And I appreciate that, Mister Tennyson. It's a frustrating case. We'll need citizen input. If you hear something or think of something, let me know."

"I will. Tell your Dad I said hello."

Marklin toasted me with his cup as he left.

I watched him walk out into the parking lot and climb into a white Crown Victoria that much too obviously was an unmarked police car.

I hadn't thought much about the dead woman for a few days. Now she was back, staring at nothing, the bullet hole in her forehead aimed straight up at the sky, like a third eye.

What had she seen in the last moments before she died?

Was her ghost with me now, standing invisibly beside me, telling me something I could not hear?

Or do we stay where we die, rooted forever to that one spot?

There were no answers and no clues at the bottom of my iced tea lemonade.

I got a refill.

THIRTEEN

Later that morning, I drove up and down Burnet Road and Lamar Boulevard, looking for "Help Wanted" and "Now Hiring" signs. There weren't many. A car wash was hiring "vacuum and drying specialists"; a Mexican restaurant needed a waitress; a Chinese restaurant wanted an "experienced" dishwasher; a hardware and appliance store wanted "part-time commission sales associates"; an animal hospital needed a "trained vet tech."

Back at my apartment, I went online again. Robert had sent me a "What's your decision?" email. I didn't answer it right away. Instead, I did a Google search, found some sites for online classes and started considering the lengthy lists of grim possibilities:
"...Accountant...Electrician...Medical Transcriptionist...Paralegal...Plumber...Private Investigator...Public Relations Specialist...Speech Therapist...Web Designer..."

Wait a minute. Private investigator. Could I do that?

I had reviewed plenty of gumshoe novels over the years.

"The new Raymond Chandler... the new Dashiell Hammett...the new Robert B. Parker...a tour de force mystery thriller packed with intrigue and heart-stopping action ... better than Marlowe, Spenser, Poirot, Sherlock Holmes <u>and</u> Miss Marple rolled into one!"

One link brought up a long list of other websites that included a $32,000 online Ph. D. in criminal justice, a $400 online "detective school" and a $50 "how to be a P.I." course that I could download and print out from a big PDF.

If I paid an extra $15, I could even receive an "official" private investigator certificate suitable for framing once I completed the assignments. No doubt it was a PDF, too. But I figured it might look okay hanging high up on a wall, in a nice frame from Michael's or CVS.

Ridiculous, I decided finally. *I can't be a P.I.*

To reaffirm that vow, I stood in front of my bathroom mirror and did a quick self-assessment. I had none of the classic tough-guy looks of detective movies and TV shows. I resembled a worn-out cross between Mister Rogers and Captain Kangaroo. My best punch would just hurt my hand. And the last time I had fired a gun was 43 years ago, in the Navy, a Model 1911 Colt .45. I had unleashed five shots and hit the outer circle of a paper target with exactly two of them.

I wanted nothing to do with guns, and I knew Joan would not want me packing any heat. I might blow off a toe. Or something much, much more vital.

A gun is just a trouble magnet, I told myself, seeing and feeling my face grimace. *Sooner or later, if you have one, you'll have to pull it and use it.*

Still, I needed to make a choice, and I needed to make it now.

I studied my chin in the mirror. I *did* have the perfect stubble for a character in a film noir detective movie.

I could be Bystander #5

Perhaps even Old Guy #6.

I left my apartment, got in my Sunfire, took a couple of back streets and turned south on Lamar, destination unknown.

I did random driving like this when I needed to clear my head of dust devils and dried-up thoughts.

At 45th and Lamar, I turned right, continued to Burnet Road, took another right in front of Upper Crust bakery and headed north.

I could borrow money and start classes next week. Austin Community College had a branch campus about five miles up the road from my apartment. In a year or so, I could have a certificate in real estate and might be good enough to barely assist Joan. Or I could focus on an "exciting new career" in something else, such as meeting and events planning or being a paralegal or fixing air conditioners.

Or, I could pay $65 for the online course, with laser-printed certificate, and become a private investigator in just 30 days.

My poor mother had had a frequent warning for me when I was young: "Erwin Tennyson, don't you go borrowing trouble."

So, okay, Mom. I won't, I mused as I drove. *I won't borrow anything.*

And I won't, I decided, waste my dwindling life savings on a certificate in personal fitness training or travel and tourism planning.

I'll be a no-fisted detective.

A sleuth and nothing but a sleuth.

A master of stealth, disguises and deduction—and staying the hell out of harm's way.

Erwin Tennyson, P.I.P.I.

Practically Invisible Private Investigator.

FOURTEEN

I sent Robert an email politely declining his offer. But I asked him to "keep me in mind if your publication's financial position improves."

His reply was quick and direct. "You just pissed away your big chance, good buddy. But okay."

While I was still at my computer, I used my MasterCard to pay $65 to the Advanced Online School of Private Investigation (AOSPI), which, true to its name, apparently had no physical offices or campus anywhere on the planet.

The confirmation email gave me the link to the textbook. It was a 327-page PDF tome covering everything from the history of private investigation to how to invoice clients and turn them over to collection agencies if they don't pay. It had been written by a South Dakota private investigator with "20 years in the business."

I clicked the "print" option, and its pages started stacking up in my printer.

The message also contained the link to the PDF certificate that I had assumed would be issued once I completed the course. I clicked on the link. A clever application already had inserted my name. The certificate read: "Having successfully completed all courses and requirements of the Advanced Online School of Private Investigation, ERWIN TENNYSON is hereby declared an official PRIVATE INVESTIGATOR and is entitled to all rights and privileges pertaining to that designation."

I could print it out now, put it in a frame and just skip the course. Many had done that, I was sure. But in my mind, that would be cheating – something only a lowlife would do. I wanted to be the type of P.I. who wore honor and dignity like a shield, or at least like a fedora and a London Fog trench coat.

I hole-punched the 327 pages and put them into a heavy-duty three-ring binder. Then I copied the link to the certificate, pasted it into a blank document, saved it, printed it out and hole-punched it. Finally, I put the sheet into the course binder, right after the page that said "The End."

Printing the certificate, I decided, would be one of my rewards for finishing the course.

"For now, I'll just practice," I said to Joan that evening. It was my turn again to host for the night, and I was serving her a plate of my famous, straight-out-of-the-box beef Stroganoff.

"I'll try some out some of the surveillance techniques and online record searches and see how well I like doing this."

"Uh huh," Joan said.

She didn't look up from her new Crate & Barrel catalogue. She often brought catalogues over to my apartment and read them while I cooked dinner. She usually left them on my kitchen table the next morning with a dog ear or Post-It Note marking a particular page I was supposed to see.

Lands' End, L.L. Bean, Eddie Bauer, Travel Smith, the Container Store...

No doubt she was trying to inspire me – if not shame me – into upgrading my wardrobe and apartment furnishings.

Gradually, I was doing that, one shirt, two pillowcases and three crab forks at a time.

"Ranch or Italian?" I said, holding up two small plates bearing fresh disks of iceberg lettuce, horizontally sliced.

"What? "She looked up at last and eyed the plates. "I'll have the creamy garlic, onion and basil vinaigrette." She returned to studying the Crate & Barrel catalogue.

"Trash cans are two dollars off this week. You need new trash cans, Erwin."

I sprinkled her lettuce with Italian, doused mine with Ranch and set the two quasi-salads on the table.

Just in time, just before she harrumphed, I remembered the new salad forks I had been encouraged to purchase. I retrieved two from the kitchen drawer and set them just to the left of our dinner forks, on top of the two carefully folded cloth dinner napkins.

There was no arguing with her about the trash cans. If I didn't rush out after breakfast tomorrow and buy them, she would buy them for me before the end of the sale and have them gift-wrapped just for fun.

In truth, my trash cans were almost the last items in my apartment that pre-dated Joan. One of them, emblazoned with seagulls and sandpipers, was a true classic. I had bought it at an old Gibson's department store in Denton, Texas, for 75 cents when I set up my first apartment as an undergraduate student in 1970. The 40 years of dents and scratches just added to its charm.

Early the next morning, Joan kissed me awake. She was already dressed and ready to leave. "I got a text message from an investor. He wants a showing at 7 o'clock," she said.

In a real estate market that now seemed all but moribund, one did not argue with sales opportunities, even at sunrise.

"Close?" I asked. I rolled out of bed and realized I was au naturel.

Joan smiled. "Clear across town," she said. "Otherwise, I'd stay and help you get up."

"I'm up! I'm up!" I said. "See? Tah-DAH!" I raised my arms and did my best imitation of a gymnast acknowledging cheers after a difficult dismount.

Joan just kept smiling and slightly lowered her gaze.

"Oh," I said. I pulled the sheet protectively in front of me. "Most of me is up."

"I left you some breakfast on the table," she said, pulling her car keys from her purse.

"Sweet. What am I having?"

"I'll give you some clues, Mister Detective. Eggs. Two."

"Scrambled?" I said.

"Exactly the same size. Hardboiled. A la Poirot."

"I hate hardboiled eggs. I won't eat them," I said.

"I know," she said. "Tah-tah." She left.

I went to the kitchen grumpy but almost hungry enough to eat two hardboiled eggs.

She had scrambled them. They were tastefully piled on my breakfast plate and decorated with two sprigs of parsley. Joan also had left a plate with three pieces of toast and a pat of real French butter, as well as a small dish with strawberry preserves. A third plate had two small pieces of fresh melon.

And hot tea was steaming in my favorite mug.

Truly it was nice to be in love.

FIFTEEN

I was sitting at my favorite Starbucks, this time at a table near the front door. It was not my favorite table, but still, it afforded me a fine view of the people coming and going, especially the young women wearing running shorts, tight jeans or the latest pre-fall office fashions.

Big Paul and Little Paul strode in together and nodded at me as they passed. They got into the morning coffee line behind several doctors, nurses and state agency workers. Almost all of the line-standers were checking their phones for messages and Facebook updates. Some of them also were looking at their watches.

One man in the middle of the line took one more look at his watch, frowned, muttered something and finally gave a gesture of frustration. He left the line, hurried outside, jumped into his dirty, black Ford Focus, started it, threw it into gear, backed out quickly – and almost collided with a dirty-black Mercedes sedan that sped into the parking from Lamar Boulevard. The woman driving the Mercedes had three white poodles inside. She slammed her brakes, and the poodles went flying, but all quickly popped up again in the back seat, seemingly unhurt. They scrambled from window to window, looking out excitedly.

What was it about Austin, I wondered, that made people drive around with cars full of dogs?

The Focus screamed out of the parking lot with its tires smoking. The woman in the Mercedes backed up carefully and turned into the just-emptied parking space. She ran inside and joined the coffee line while her three dogs stood up in the rear seat and watched her through the rear window.

In front of me on my table, I had a notepad, a pen and an almost-empty iced tea lemonade cup. I was supposed to be writing a 500-word essay for my online course, spelling out why I wanted to be a private investigator. I had been at Starbucks for nearly an hour, and the notepad was still blank except for the letter "W" and a few random squiggles.

Big Paul handed me a fresh iced tea lemonade and sat down with his coffee. Little Paul stood with his mocha, dressed and armed, ready for work.

"I still don't have a book review job," I said to Big Paul.

He grinned. "Someday you will, and you'll owe me big time."

"That's bribery," I said.

"Of course it is," Big Paul said.

"And you're a witness," I said to Little Paul.

He just smirked, and we all watched a woman in her late thirties teeter past on five-inch heels. She was wearing a tight, short black skirt and an equally tight white blouse. She was carrying a cardboard tray full of drinks, no doubt for her office.

"That's one way to keep a job, I guess," Little Paul said.

Big Paul nodded. "In this economy, you gotta do what you gotta do." He took a drink of his coffee. "I'm damned glad I'm retired."

"Me, too," I said. I looked up at Little Paul. "How's the case going?"

"Which one? I got ten new ones this week."

"That many murders?" I said, shocked. Was our beloved Slacker City suddenly turning into America's murder capitol?

Little Paul laughed. "No, Mister Tennyson. Just a bunch of burglaries, missing persons, gang activities and art thefts. And a truly slimy sex offender case."

"What about the woman in the park – that case?"

Little Paul took a long drink of his mocha and sat down at our table. He seemed again to be mentally flipping through file folders.

"Still a Jane Doe suicide," he said finally. "And that's the way it's gonna stay, I guess. Too many other cases."

"Too bad," I said. I was surprised at how much her death still bothered me. Maybe she really had been a druggie or a whore, as Mister Granola had insinuated. Maybe she was an illegal immigrant. Still, somewhere, sometime, she had had a family; she had been somebody's daughter. A mother, father, sister, cousin – somebody needed to know she was dead. She deserved some kind of marker bearing her name. Not just a number in a pauper's grave.

I wanted to tell the two Pauls that I was now studying to be a P.I. But I figured I would just embarrass myself and draw some scorn. I decided to keep it secret at least until I had my diploma in hand. Or even until after I had solved my first case.

Better a rookie than a wannabe.

SIXTEEN

Little Paul took his half-finished mocha and headed off to the police station and another day of fighting crime.

Big Paul and I sat in Starbucks for another half hour, sipping our drinks, and talking about mystery writing. He turned out to be an ardent fan of the late Robert B. Parker's Boston private eye, Spenser. The guy who, in nearly thirty novels, never tells anyone his first name.

"Don't you just love it," Big Paul said, "when Spenser walks into a room and gets in a bad guy's face? The bad guy always tells *his* bad guy to beat Spenser up. Then there's a fist fight – *Biff! Pow! Bam!* – and Spenser leaves a gorilla that's twice his size unconscious on the floor with a bloody, flattened nose and broken jaw."

"Is that the kind of hero you'll have in your novel?" I said.

"No," Big Paul said. "Absolutely not. I can't top Spenser. My protagonist, Bobby Jack Dangerfield, is a bit of a stranger among the Rangers. He can shoot a gun; he can throw a fist; he can even do a triple-expresso take-down – yes, when he absolutely has to. But he'd rather confront you first with poetry."

"Poetry?"

"And the King James Bible. *And* sometimes a little Shakespeare."

"Wow."

I didn't mention that I could now hear the ghosts of book reviewers past, present and future spinning furiously in their graves.

"He's a preacher's kid, like me," Big Paul said. "His Daddy wanted him to go into the ministry, just like my Daddy did. But Bobby Jack is a bit of a rebel. He runs off to Sam Houston State University and gets a degree in criminal justice, with a minor in English. And even after he joins the Texas Rangers, he wishes he had majored in English."

"So he shoots you with poetry first and asks questions later," I said, trying to make a gentle book reviewer's joke.

Big Paul looked at me sharply. "No, no. Absolutely not. Sometimes, if he has to, he'll shoot you first and *then* quote some Sylvia Plath, *Othello*, or Paul's letters to the Corinthians – as you lay dying."

"Like William Faulkner," I said.

"Exactly. *As I Lay Dying.*"

Big Paul chuckled and smiled the smile of a man who was sure he had just found a kindred spirit. "I like you, Erwin," he said. "You *understand* what I'm trying to do."

I understood that his novel had little to no chance of getting published unless he published it himself. But I kept that grim fact to myself. In truth, I felt that I, too, had stumbled upon a kindred spirit. Big Paul had *investigated. Researched. Gathered facts.* Helped *solve* real mysteries and crimes.

If I helped him with his book, maybe he would help me find the young girl's killer.

"Well, I've read a lot of mystery novels," I said. "One hell of a lot of mystery novels."

Big Paul told me a bit more about his novel's hero, Texas Ranger Bobby Jack Thornton, and the ghost-like serial killer he keeps chasing.

I told him a bit about how I had once thought – just *thought* – of becoming a private investigator. I didn't tell him that I was now enrolled in a detective school.

Wait until you have the P.I. diploma actually and honestly in hand, I vowed again inside my head.

He nodded absently. His expression said he was still listening to his own words inside his head.

I bought us a round of refills: straight black coffee for Big Paul, iced tea lemonade for me. We kept talking about books and writing and police work for another hour.

Sometimes, in quiet tribute to T.S. Eliot, we stopped for a few moments to enjoy our drinks and just watch the people – especially the nice-looking women – come and go.

None of them talked of Michelangelo.

But a few of them did have a caramel macchiato.

SEVENTEEN

Two weeks into my private detective studies, I finally convinced Joan to help me practice the fine art of tailing a vehicle with two cars. My Social Security check had just been direct-deposited, so I boldly promised her a trip to the downtown Truluck's for seafood once we finished the exercise.

I took the lead in my Sunfire and watched the odometer's digits surge past 164,500 miles as we swept out onto MoPac Expressway from Caesar Chavez Boulevard.

Joan was a safe distance behind me, calmly tooling along in her tastefully appointed, freshly washed and spotlessly vacuumed 2011 Infiniti.

"A clean, new car instills buyer confidence when I drive clients and prospects around." That's how she once explained it to me. *"Sometimes, they have their checkbooks out and ready even before we arrive at the property."*

"Tell me again, who are we following?" she said in my cell phone.

I could barely hear her over the Sunfire's air conditioner, wind noises and tire noises, as well as the assorted squeaks and rattles of its well-earned maturity.

I scanned the traffic ahead and picked out a target.

"Grey Honda Element, center lane, right in front of me."

I shifted into my best police dispatcher/military radio operator voice. "License number Bravo, Whiskey, Romeo, Charlie, five, niner, niner, three."

"You mean the car with the purple bumper sticker," she said.

She was right, of course.

"I'm going to change lanes and drop back a little," I said. "Move up a bit and stay on her tail."

"I can see her just fine from here."

"Don't lose her."

"Roger, dodger. Wilco and over."

"It's 'wilco, out,'" I said. "You need to watch more World War II airplane movies."

"I'd rather watch you bail out of your pants," Joan said.

The Honda Element's driver gave no hint that she realized she was being followed.

We started getting close to the spot where MoPac splits into a "Y".

I tried to deduce what our "suspect" would do next.

If she stayed to the right on MoPac, she would head north toward Braker Lane, Duval Road, West Parmer Lane and points north. If she moved to the left soon, she would drive through Research Boulevard's retail areas and head northwest toward Anderson Mill Road, the Texas 45 toll road, and suburban Cedar Park.

She stayed right as the "Y" approached.

"Okay, Joan, move up and stay close," I said into my phone. "I'll move ahead of her for a while."

No response.

"Joan? Joan? Move up!" I said.

65

I looked in my rear-view mirror and saw Joan's well-waxed Infiniti. It was now heading left toward Highway 183. "Wrong way! Wrong way!" I said.

No response.

Suddenly, she was back on the line. "Sorry, Erwin," she said. "I got a text message. There's a three-hour sale at the Container Store. Twenty-five percent off. I need a couple of small shelves for a house staging."

"Okay," I said, miffed. "Bye."

"Yes, I will buy. And we can go Dutch tonight at Truluck's," Joan said. She hung up.

I tailed the "suspect" for another two miles. But as we approached the Duval Road exit, I lost interest in keeping up the game. She might drive her Honda Element all the way to Pflugerville, Georgetown, Temple or Waco. Or, God forbid, Dallas.

From Duval, I merged onto Burnet Road and headed south, passing long strings of small businesses and occasional empty store fronts and shops with signs: "Closing Sale"; "Everything Must Go"; "70% Off All Merchandise." For a select few in America's economy, these were – if not the best of times – at least some pretty good times. But their prosperity wasn't trickling down.

At the traffic light at Burnet Road and North Loop, I suddenly thought of the dead woman again and wished I could come up with a clue, any clue, that might help Sgt. Marklin identify her.

My mind remained frustratingly blank as the signal changed from red to green.

I moved on with the traffic flow, not really sure where I was going, except further south.

EIGHTEEN

"I just have to tail somebody for a while and gather as much information about them as I can," I said. "It'll be good exercise."

Following a suspect on foot was my next lesson in how to be a private eye.

Joan shook her head no, adamant.

"I have better things to do with my life and time," she said. "*Many* better things."

"You could hold my hand and keep me from looking like some kind of pervert," I said.

"No."

"Did I hear a 'maybe' somewhere in that 'no'?"

"You heard 'no,' Erwin, everywhere in that 'no.'"

One did not easily argue with Joan Larson, aggressive Austin real-estate agent and well-coiffed Infiniti driver.

She left her house to start another day in the exciting, adventure-packed world of selling and buying high-dollar West Austin properties.

Meanwhile, I loaded and started her dishwasher. Then I tackled the changing the sheets and making up her big bed.

The king-sized, fitted sheet was the toughest challenge. I had to get the first elasticized corner to quit popping up when I stretched the 1500-thread-count Egyptian cotton fabric toward the second corner. It was never a problem, of course, when Joan and I worked together.

Still, I knew how to be inventive in a pinch. In her neatly organized utility room, I found an almost-full roll of blue painter's tape.

I took it to the bedroom and taped down the bottom edge of the sheet's first corner once it was in place. The tape held while I stretched the sheet and hooked the second corner over the mattress. After that, corners three and four were a snap. I removed the tape pieces, making absolutely sure I left behind no evidence of my technique.

I didn't want Joan to think I was helpless without her.

Fifteen minutes later, I finished smoothing out the huge bedspread and positioning all of the various practical and decorative pillows.

Now I opened her main closet and studied my small gathering of clothing almost hidden at one end. What would a well-dressed Austin private eye wear while following somebody in basic gumshoe mode?

Joan and I both liked Renaissance and baroque music, so the FM radios in her various rooms all played the same soothing classical sounds while I checked through my choices. The weather report, spoken calmly between two *concerti grossi* on KMFA, was predictable for August: clear and hot, with an afternoon high of 103.

I settled for the "Austin area man" look, as Joan jokingly termed it. Tan cargo shorts with some of the pockets left unsnapped; a faded black South by Southwest film festival T-shirt worn tail-out; a grey baseball cap with black bill; and well-scuffed running shoes worn with grey, topless socks.

Just as I stuffed my wallet and keys into a pocket, my candy-bar cell phone rang.

"Joan," the display flashed.

I sensed she was calling to apologize for not agreeing to help me follow someone. I was sure she had decided to reconsider.

"Don't forget we're going to a dinner party tonight," she said.

She heard the hesitation in my silence.

"You forgot, didn't you? Six-thirty. I'm driving."

I still had no idea what I had agreed to do.

But she could read my thought processes, too. Especially when I had no idea what I was supposed to be thinking.

"Just to recap, Erwin, we're getting together tonight for a dinner party. We'll be with some of my friends from my two favorite title companies. You'll wear your dark suit, a white shirt and that lovely blue tie I got you last summer. Okay?"

"Got it," I said. "White suit, blue shirt, dark tie."

I was trying to be funny, but clearly, I wasn't faking enough real enthusiasm.

"Most of the jokes and small talk," Joan said, "will be about real estate, money and UT football. We'll leave the party precisely at eight-thirty and go straight to your place. Then I'll calmly and very carefully rip off your clothes."

"That sounds like fun," I said, unable now to subdue my enthusiasm.

"It's my idea of fun, too," Joan said.

NINETEEN

The next day, I considered following someone through a shopping mall. It would be easy there, I figured, to pick out an unsuspecting surveillance target and remain inconspicuous among the shoppers.

But I hated going to malls, especially alone. And the information I could gather would be minimal at best: appearance, clothing, what stores visited, what merchandise and fast-food items purchased, which hand used when depositing trash in a receptacle.

I drove to a medical tower, instead. One of those six-story rectangular glass boxes with many different doctors' offices inside. The parking lot was almost full. A lot of people were sick today or getting treatments and checkups.

I parked in the outer ring of vehicles and got out. Some of the "Compact Car Only" spaces had brand-new Chevy Suburbans and Toyota Tundras parked in them. They were parked so they took up two "Compact Car Only" spaces and left plenty of room to avoid dings from other drivers' doors.

Where, I wondered, were the parking lot cops when you really needed them?

It crossed my mind that I could go over and kick in some big dents. Mete out Old West justice on behalf of the oppressed compact-car drivers who had to keep circling and circling in hopes of finding a free space. But I knew if I really did dent a door, *then* the parking-lot police would show up full force and catch me red-footed.

As I stood watching the parking lot, a woman driving a big white Ford F250 pickup truck pulled in not far away and parked at an angle across two regular-sized slots. The truck's bumper had two bumper stickers: "Nobama Care" and "Liberals Suck." Clearly, she wasn't from around here – "here" being central Travis County, the liberal heart of Texas.

She climbed down from her behemoth truck and walked toward the medical building, talking the whole way on her pink cell phone. I tried discreetly to make legible notes in a little notebook as I followed her. She was dressed in tight, blue designer jeans that accented and rounded her nice ass. She had on a Western-style white blouse with cactus floral patterns and a sprinkling of rhinestones that shimmered and sparkled in the sunlight. She was also wearing a wide, rodeo cowgirl-style, dark- tan leather belt. She walked along on flat little sandals that barely showed up on her feet. And her hair was pulled back in a long, light-brown pony tail that swished back and forth just above her waist.

I followed her into the medical building and stood by her while she and two other women waited for an elevator.

She was still talking into her cell phone.

"And then I told him, no, like, that's not how it's done. And then he said like yes it is. And I said like no. And he like tried to like argue, and that's when I like told him to, like, you know, go to hell."

The elevator dinged its arrival and the door opened. I stepped up first and held the door open while my surveillance subject and the others stepped in.

She kept talking for a moment, oblivious to the others around her. "And then he like tried to argue with me but – hello? Hello?"

She pulled her phone away from her face and glared at it.

"No bars in here, I bet," I said.

She stuffed her phone in a jeans pocket. "Six, please," she said.

I punched the floor button. "I'm going there, too," I said.

She said nothing. Her mind clearly was still on the phone and her unfinished conversation.

As I followed her off the elevator, I hoped she wasn't going in to see a gynecologist. That would be the end of the surveillance trail for this gumshoe cowboy.

She wasn't. She entered an office that had six names on the door, all in family medicine and general practice. I tried to memorize the names but didn't have time. I followed her in and grabbed a worn copy of *People* magazine from a table. I stood looking at it with apparently rapt interest while she announced that she had a ten-thirty appointment with Doctor Smithers. The receptionist handed her a clipboard full of forms to fill out, and when she sat down, I sat down beside her. The magazine was so old, some of its cover celebrities had been dead for at least two years.

The receptionist looked out at me, checked her clipboard, and slid open her little window. "Sir, who are you here to see?"

"I'm early," I said, thinking fast. "I'm here to meet someone who's coming in later for a consultation."

The receptionist looked at the clipboard again. "Mrs. Wyman at eleven o'clock with Doctor Cantrell?"

"That's the one," I said, smiling.

She smiled back at me and closed her window again.

Meanwhile, my surveillance subject was putting in her confidential information right beside me. I pulled the entertainment magazine back up to my face, but turned my head slightly so I could look down at what she was writing.

It shouldn't be this easy, I thought.

I started to get up and leave. But I made myself stick with the "investigation." I pulled out my pen and little pocket notebook and pretended to copy some information from inside the magazine. What I wrote down, however, was her name, address, telephone number, Social Security number and driver's license number. The number on her insurance card was too long to write down, and now her hand now covered part of it as she changed her grip on the clipboard.

She checked "abdominal cramps" as one of her symptoms, but I didn't write that down. I decided I had done more than enough work for the foot surveillance lesson.

I returned the magazine to the magazine table and casually strolled out the door.

Back home, I did a Google search and quickly found Mandee Blintlikoff's Facebook page and her "Mandee's Tea Party" blog. She was, indeed, a hater of political and social liberals everywhere, in any shape and form. And her web pages made more of her personal information available for easy picking.

It bothered me how easy it was to spy on people, steal their details and use them to mess up their lives.

I tore the sheets out of my notebook and fed them one at a time into my diamond-cut paper shredder.

The little pieces fluttered down to the bottom like snow.

TWENTY

In most private-eye mystery novels, there is little or no focus on *how* the burnt-out, booze-soaked hero became an investigator.

Usually, he is just an ex-cop who got into big trouble on the job or ran afoul of corrupt higher-ups and ended up getting fired. He doesn't want to change careers and become Spenser, accountant, or Phillip Marlowe, X-ray technician.

The search for truth and justice and the way of the fist and gun are all he really understands.

Meanwhile, the *process* he has followed to become a P.I. hardly matters.

To the bitter or frightened damsel in distress, it only matters that he is a two-fisted knight-errant with a snub-nosed .38, whiskey breath and a day-old beard.

I figured it would be easy to set up a P.I. practice in Texas. Just fill out a simple form; pay a small fee; hang a modest shingle on the wall.

That was the process for opening almost any kind of small business in the state that still embodied the Wild West. Texas had always been a happy home for slick operators who hated taxes, bureaucracy, restrictions and regulations.

"How hard could it be?" I said to Joan.

She slid a mystery dinner into my tiny microwave and pushed the "Start" button.

"Have you actually checked?" she said.

She had stopped by just after noon, hoping I would take her out to Wendy's, Whataburger, McDonald's or some other quick bistro where she could get a chicken Caesar salad in a plastic to-go box. She had another house showing in 45 minutes, and she looked absolutely smashing in her real-estate-lady clothes that didn't exactly hide her legs and cleavage.

But I was busy taking the final exam in my online class. Just five more multiple-choice questions to go, all dealing with what a suspect might do if he or she realized someone was tailing them. "Sometimes speed up or slow down...cut through a parking lot...go through a restaurant drive-through...pull into a driveway...head out onto a congested freeway."

While I pondered the potential answers and clicked on my choices, I could hear Joan working behind me, making plate and cutlery noises on the counter.

My laptop's screen flashed "Course Completed!" in big letters, and a tinny but triumphant fanfare briefly played as a new message screen popped up.

"Congratulations! Print out your Official Private Investigator Certificate now!"

While the laser printer clacked and whirred, I turned in my chair, raised my fists in victory and grinned at Joan.

"You are now dating a private investigator!" I said.

She contained her joy very carefully.

"Come eat your chicken whatzit," she said.

She dumped the contents of both microwave meals onto the two nice china plates she had loaned me soon after we started dating.

My lunch was noodles, vegetable pieces and little chicken chunks lying in some kind of quasi-Oriental sauce. Hers was a veggie delight: a large, tastefully arranged glop of butternut squash, carrots, onions and broccoli.

I held my new certificate and admired it while I forked up some of the chicken conglomeration. Only a couple of noodles missed my mouth and landed on my pants.

Joan finished her lunch quickly, checked her watch and stepped over to my computer.

"I won't get a gun. That's a promise," I said as I finished off the final noodles.

Joan scrolled and paged quickly through some screen displays.

"And I won't get us into any kind of danger. I'll just sneak around, observe, take notes, take pictures, write reports, and turn over all evidence to those who can do something about it."

A website now was visible on my computer screen.

"You might want to take a look at this," Joan said. "Gotta go."

She gave me a quick kiss. "Dinner at my place, six o'clock. T-bone steaks. Don't forget your jammies and bunny slippers."

I gave her my best detective leer and snarl. "You got it, doll face."

Joan cocked her head and stared at me for a moment. "Call me doll face one more time, Erwin Tennyson, and I'll walk your gumshoes straight down your throat. That's a solemn promise."

"I love you, too!" I called after her as she left.

TWENTY-ONE

I recycled the lunch plastic and cleaned off the table. Then I went to my computer and looked at the state government screen Joan had left up.

Bureaucracy, it appeared, now ruled the Wild West.

The Texas Department of Safety's website stated sternly that anyone wanting to be a P.I. in the Lone Star State absolutely must register with the Private Security Bureau.

I could do that, I figured. Probably online.

But it further stated that there were only three valid ways to get a Texas private investigator's license: (1) work for a licensed P.I. company; (2) have full-time experience as a peace officer or insurance investigator; or (3) show proof that you have a four-year criminal justice degree from an accredited university or college.

My fresh, new PDF diploma from the Advanced Online School of Private Investigation was worthless. Less than worthless. My career as a P.I. was over before it had even started.

I took my laptop to Starbucks, sat glumly at my favorite table, and surfed the web while I absently drank some passion tea lemonade for a change. I was nearly halfway through the drink before I realized I had forgotten to put any Splenda in it.

What would my *next* avocation be?

I found another website and started pondering its long list of possibilities: "…aircraft mechanic…chef…investment counselor…pest control technician…veterinary assistant…"

None of these sounded the least bit interesting.

I decided I needed a drink – a *real* drink.

I called Frank Arkandale, an old friend who had worked with me for five years at the now-departed *Dallas Times Herald.*

In his early days as a newspaper journalist, Frank had been a keen practitioner of the fine art of melting into crowds, blending into backgrounds and otherwise *not* standing out. He was medium height and medium weight and, in those days, always kept his hair cut medium length. He wore muted colors and consistently championed journalistic objectivity. "Reporters must stand back, observe and *report*," he used to insist to me. "We must never become *participants* in the events and news we cover."

That had all changed quickly after he sold his first novel, *6Gun*, a gritty Western that hit the *New York Times* best-seller list. He quit the newspaper game, penned a second Western best seller, *6Gun Returns*, and soon became well-known, nationally and internationally, for his off-the-wall fashion statements.

Television interviewers who expected him to show up wearing rodeo garb were startled and thrown off stride when he arrived dressed in a tuxedo or toga or even the tight garb of a toreador. Soon, famous talk-show hosts began inviting him to their programs, and they started hyping his scheduled appearance by inviting viewers to phone in and speculate on what "Frank Arkandale, the Elton John of best-selling cowboy novelists" might wear this time when he was introduced.

One night, 20 million late-night viewers had tuned in to see Frank talk about his latest book, best-seller number three, *Pilgrim with a Pistol*. The top two guesses for his costume had been "New England Pilgrim with a 10-gallon hat" and "Apache warrior armed with a bazooka." Frank stunned and disappointed everyone by stepping into the spotlight dressed like a Harvard economics professor, and the show quickly lost ten million viewers, the Associated Press reported the next morning.

Now in his late sixties, with at least twenty best-sellers to his credit and a fortune in royalties to spend, Frank no longer did book promotional appearances. And he had settled into one convenient and inexpensive fashion statement that never seemed to change: faded blue jeans, faded denim shirt and worn brown leather sandals. His hair, completely white now, was kept pulled back into a pony tail that reached almost to the middle of his back.

Frank had been something of a mentor to me when I was fresh out of journalism school and still trying to fathom the alleged joys of being a reporter assigned to cover suburban city council meetings.

He had graduated two years ahead of me and already had won three awards for reporting when he taught me the importance of focusing intently on the task at hand without really giving a shit about what I was doing.

What he had *not* told me then was that he was writing Western novels on the side. Two days after *6Gun* sold, he quit the *Times Herald* and relocated to Austin. "It's one of the most *literary* cities in America," he told me as he cleaned out his desk. "Dallas and Houston are just all about making *money*."

Despite that disdain, Frank now was rich several times over. And, after his long string of commercial successes and a Western Writers of America award, he had transitioned with apparently amazing ease into writing science-fiction fantasy novels.

The *Austin Chronicle* had just named Frank Arkandale "Austin's best science-fiction novelist" for the fourth year in a row.

His latest book, *High Noon on Neptune*, was entering its fourteenth week on the *New York Times* best seller list. According to *Variety*, he also had just sold the movie rights to an unnamed studio for an undisclosed seven-figure amount.

Years ago, before I got locked into reviewing mystery novels, I had reviewed the first two of Frank's paperback oaters that followed his *6Gun* series. They were written fairly well, but I didn't particularly care for his new hero, Deputy Marshal Ben Joseph, who always seemed to be the only guy with guts and goodness in Wilbarger County. His few friends called him "Ben Joe," which always reminded me of *benjo*, Japanese slang for "toilet." And his main flaw – aside from an unstoppable passion for justice --was gambling. He gambled away his pay, he gambled with women – particularly by trying to have more than one relationship at a time. And he foolishly gambled with his life each time he went up against an evil gang, completely outgunned.

"I don't feel like driving to a bar right now," Frank said when I called him. "Get us some Shiner and come on out to the *hacienda.*"

TWENTY-TWO

Frank's hacienda was exactly that: a substantial estate. He owned a very large spread of very expensive ranchland six miles west of Austin, and his huge, adobe-colored two-story house was perched atop a hill situated almost in its center.

The hill had been there when Frank bought the land fifteen years ago. But when it proved too small for the house he envisioned, he had brought in earthmoving equipment and tons of dirt and paid nearly a million dollars to have the hill tripled in size.

His shaded second-story patio offered a commanding view of the Texas Hill Country, Lake Travis and far horizons, as well as his micro-herd of eleven Longhorn steers now clustered a few hundred yards away in the shade of a hundred-year-old oak tree.

Having cattle on his land qualified him for state and federal agricultural tax breaks. Beyond that, he paid the steers little attention. He left their care to a rural cowhand who stopped by twice a day to feed and water the animals and fix any breaks in his very lengthy barbed-wire fence.

We sat at a table and ate tortilla chips while we worked our way through the Shiner, an old-time Texas beer.

After a while, I told him about my foundering attempts to become a private investigator.

"Er," he said.

Years ago, Frank had quit calling me "Erwin" and settled irritatingly on "Er."

"Er, you've read a *million* detective novels. You should write one."

"I've never written anything longer than a magazine article," I said. It was the truth.

"Excuses, excuses. A page a day is a book a year. You know that."

He bit into another chip and soaked it with a sip of beer. "Write three pages a day, and you'll finish a detective novel in four months. Maybe sooner."

"I don't know anything about writing fiction," I said.

"What's to know? Just make things up." Frank took a long pull from his beer bottle and held the amber glass up to the sun so he could check the liquid level. "Give your detective a character flaw – booze, sex, money, power, gambling, cross-dressing, something like that – and make it keep getting in the way of his investigations."

I didn't know much about character flaws, either. Not really. Joan sometimes jokingly accused me of being "an overgrown Boy Scout" and "a goody three shoes," which, she pointed out, was "fifty percent worse than being a goody two shoes."

But she always added that my "cute ass" more than made up for any of these deficits.

I didn't tell Frank that.

He finished off his beer and popped open another one.

"What if my detective is completely normal?" I said. "Nobody has done that. In today's messed-up world, you're flawed if you're normal."

Frank smirked.

"Er," he said, "normal is *dull*." He took a long pull from long-neck bottle. "Nobody would publish it. And nobody would buy it. *Nobody* wants to read about a *normal* detective. Me, especially."

We munched a few more chips and drank in silence now.

A hawk circled lazily overhead, riding the afternoon thermal currents. A 737 swept in from the northwest, likely from Midland-Odessa, heading for Austin-Bergstrom International Airport.

I felt a lightness, like helium, beginning to rise inside my head.

My brain, in fact, felt as if it was losing weight and now in danger of simply floating away.

If I wrote fiction, *where* would I start? And *what* would I *say*?

Did I, in fact, have *anything* to say?

TWENTY-THREE

After one more beer and another half bowl of chips, I told Frank about discovering the dead woman in the park and watching the police investigate the scene.

Her death, I told him, might make the start of a good mystery story.

By now, I was just loose-tongued and talking to hear my head rattle, as my mother used to say. I had no actual clue what I might write about the woman in the park.

Frank seemed to listen attentively for a moment. Then he grinned. "No mystery in that case, Er," he said dismissively. "The medical examiner ruled it a suicide."

"Really?" I said. "When?"

He picked up a folded *Daily Democrat* from a corner of the big patio table and tossed it to me.

"Metro section, page three, down near the bottom."

I checked. Her autopsy had revealed gunshot residue on her left hand. Police were still seeking the gun "presumed stolen from the scene." She remained unidentified.

Frank looked right at me, the way he had at the *Times Herald* when he was imparting the wisdom of his greater experience. "I still read newspapers cover to cover every morning, Er," he told me now. "Headlines, obits, sports notes; hell, even the classifieds. I get a lot of ideas for fiction from newspapers."

He turned up his beer and chugged the last few swallows.

"But I also try to go out somewhere every day and experience *life*," he said. He gestured grandly with his empty bottle. "I *do* things so I can write about them *knowledgeably*."

He had enough of a buzz going now that he had to carefully pronounce each syllable of the word.

He pulled the last Shiner from the carton, popped its top and took a long pull from its amber bottle.

"The stuff of fiction is all around you in real life. Find it. Steal it. Grab it by the throat. Kick it in the butt. Hell, shoot it in the head. Whatever, Er. Get your material wherever and however you can and *use* it. Write it down."

"Then it's simple," I said, now completely loose of tongue. "To Er is human, and a book a day is a page a year."

I knew from his facial expression that Frank now was listening to nothing but the inside of his own head.

"Fuckin'-A," he said finally, staring off into the distance.

It was no fun tripping him up when he didn't even realize he had been tripped.

The dead woman stayed on my mind as I drove away from Frank's hacienda near sunset. At the fancy fence line, I stopped at the cattle guard and waited for the electric gate to open. Frank's eleven Longhorns did not stampede and try to escape. They remained almost motionless under the big oak tree, no doubt thinking deep steer thoughts.

At the end of Frank's long driveway, I turned onto the Farm-to-Market road that led back toward downtown Austin. In my rear view mirror, I watched the electric gate swing closed behind me and lock.

Now I focused on the hilly, winding road ahead. Many of the simple Hill Country peasants liked to drive their Jaguars, Beamers and Lincoln Navigators too fast while TWI'ing – texting or Tweeting while intoxicated. Once in a while, there were $200,000 head-on collisions and "OMG!" fatalities.

I was merely driving while intoxicated. But my brain slowly began to function again as I focused on the asphalt ahead and the painted lines and the potholes.

Why would someone with so much life ahead fire a gun into her forehead? And why near an Austin city park's running path? No car had been left behind, unclaimed. She had not driven there.

Why had she *not* left behind some sense of who she was and why she was ending her life?

It was murder, plain and simple.

Or, it was murder, ambiguous and complex.

In truth, I had no idea what it was.

But I knew I wanted to find out.

For no clear reason I could discern or understand, I wanted to know *why* that young woman had died. And if someone had killed her, I wanted him or her to pay – *something* – for the crime.

There had to be a price. There had to be justice.

There *had* to be.

Didn't there?

TWENTY-FOUR

A few hours before dawn, a minimal tropical storm came ashore 200 miles south of Austin. Now it was raining cats, if not quite dogs.

It was just after nine a.m. Joan had left without waking me.

But her note on the kitchen counter reminded me to eat a bowl of oatmeal "and have a glass of milk and some other protein. See you at my place at six."

She had underlined the word "protein" twice and added a little postscript at the edge of the note: "You'll need it!"

I opened the green curtains that covered the sliding door to my balcony. The cactus was getting drenched. And black ashes were draining out from the flooded little hibachi. The trees just looked olive-drab under the grey sky. I did not feel inspired. And I did not feel hungry.

I stepped away from the glass door and looked at my framed certificate from the Advanced Online School of Private Investigation. Why had I thought I could actually investigate something and figure it out? And, more importantly, why had I thought I could *do* something about it?

I was not a real detective. On days like this, I should just sit in a rocking chair, collect my Social Security check, and read mystery novels. I could be a vicarious detective with none of the confusions, worries and risks. Joan had loved me before I started this crazy quest, and she would still love me if I stopped.

I *could* write a mystery novel. Joan would love that. Perhaps I could create a private detective who made Sherlock Holmes seem like a mental midget or Mickey Spillane's hard-fisted Mike Hammer resemble a stale creampuff.

A Glock Gothic, Smith & Wesson suspense story.

There was one small hitch. Certificate or no, I didn't actually *know* how private investigators worked. I couldn't really walk the walk. I couldn't really talk the talk. None of that had been covered in the online class.

And nobody seemed to need a "private researcher" at the moment.

I sat down at my kitchen table and stared at the screensaver star fields moving across my laptop computer's 15-inch screen.

I had plenty of time to think.

Maybe the woman had been pursued by someone who shot her and took every identifying item off her body before making his – or her – escape.

I didn't think a woman would shoot another woman square in the forehead. A guy – some sort of soulless, heartless, brainless loser – might do that, but a woman was much less likely. I imagined she would take a step or two back and shoot for the heart or stomach, not the head.

What if it had been a random robbery, and the thief had decided to eliminate the only witness?

Maybe she had an incurable disease and couldn't face the pain. And she couldn't bear to kill herself, so she had a friend shoot her.

I called Marklin and told him that last theory.

"Who?" He seemed confused.

"The woman in the park."

"That was three, four deaths ago," he said. He sounded a bit harried. "We've filed it as a Jane Doe suicide and moved on."

"Suicide? I'm thinking it was murder," I said.

I realized suddenly that I was attempting to speak to him detective to detective, P.I. to city, Spenser to Belton.

In reality, it was guy-with-a-PDF-diploma to *actual* detective, duly licensed, sworn, trained and experienced at investigations.

"Do you have something new?" He sounded both alert and irritated now.

"I'm just a concerned citizen trying to help." I said, retreating quickly.

"*Why* are you still concerned?" Marklin said.

"I don't know. She was young enough to be my daughter. She was somebody's kid."

"Everybody that's dead was somebody's kid," Marklin said.

I heard him blow out his breath. His voice and attitude audibly softened. "Hang on a minute."

I heard him put the phone down. There were a few muffled voices in the background. A filing cabinet drawer was opened and then closed after a few seconds.

Marklin picked up the phone again. "Coroner says she was healthier than any of us."

"Except for the bullet hole in her head."

"That's right."

"What caliber?"

I heard Marklin start to answer. Then he hesitated and sucked in his breath. "Are you *investigating* this?"

I was sharp enough to pick up his emphasis. I would have to be very careful with my answer.

"I'm thinking I may do like your Dad and write a novel," I said. "I need to know how things work."

This seemed to satisfy him. "All right, caliber. Let's see, forty, forty-four, forty-five – hard to tell. Makes little difference at that range. Vic's head explodes."

"Who's Vic?"

Marklin chuckled. "The vic. The victim. It's how we talk on the job."

I told Marklin I'd like to buy him lunch sometime. "In return for more information about what it's like to be a detective."

"Okay," he said. "But you really should talk with Dad. He's the one with free time."

Soon after we hung up, a lightning bolt suddenly split the sky, and thunder rattled my apartment's patio window. I got up from the table and watched the rain for a while.

It was now a noir kind of day, and I was very much in a noir mood. I considered getting online and watching *The Maltese Falcon* on Netflix.

Instead, I checked my email and found nothing of interest. Then I drifted into random Google searches and started following distracting links.

I could be a private researcher without leaving my kitchen table. But I couldn't be a private detective disguised as a private researcher unless I had an office.

And the seedier it is, the better, I vowed.

The sky darkened even more. The rain fell harder.

Somehow, this seemed more an affirmation than a warning sign from the gods.

I moved my mouse and got on Craigslist.

TWENTY-FIVE

Almost right away, I found "a Great Recession move-in special, first month free with six-month lease."

Sounded exactly like my kind of place. Early the next morning, I drove over to see it and signed the lease twenty minutes after I got there.

For $390 a month, I now had a ten-by-ten "executive suite" in a block-long, rectangular building jam-packed with dozens of other ten-by-tens, all fronting a not-so-busy Austin side street.

"A business incubator," its flyer had hailed it. Right now, it looked more like a bankruptcy incubator. Most of the flanking office spaces had big "For Lease" signs in their windows. But what the hell. "Erwin Tennyson, Specialized Researcher" was now open business. And it would not be difficult to change the name to "Erwin Tennyson, Private Investigator" if I figured out how to get over the sticky hurdle of needing a state license.

It was shaping up to be my lucky day. The previous occupant of my office space had left behind a battered black computer desk and an olive-drab filing cabinet that appeared to have miraculously survived Desert Storm.

The leasing agent's little bronze name tag said "Karen." She was a tall, willowy, twentysomething blonde made even taller – basketball tall – by her classic black pumps with four-inch heels. She had to duck slightly as she entered my new headquarters.

"What used to be in here?" I said as Karen gave me a copy of my lease agreement and my key to the front door.

"Let's see." She flashed perfectly straight, perfectly brilliant teeth as she checked her clipboard.

In my investigative cleverness, I had scanned her long list of available offices and selected number B221. Only the truest fans of detective fiction would recognize it as a clever homage to Sherlock Holmes' street address, 221-B Baker Street.

"Here it is," Karen said. "A private investigator had this office."

Of course, I thought. *An excellent omen.*

"He left us owing two months' rent."

Oops.

Karen glanced around at the blank, off-white walls and the light-yellow tile ceiling. She made a few checkmarks on another form on her clipboard. Now she looked up at me and flashed her light-reflecting teeth again.

"What does your business do, Mister Tennyson?"

In crime fiction, this would be the point where the detective tells the girl: "Call me Erwin." But I liked being called "Mister Tennyson."

They call me Mister Tibbs...They call me Mister Tennyson...in the heat of the night.

Anyway, Joan was all the woman I could handle. And Karen appeared barely old enough to be my youngest daughter.

I hated dirty old men. But I could still glance. And admire.

"I'm in the research business," I said.

"Cool. Like science?"

I nodded. "I research certain types of human behavior."

"Oh, like a shrink!" she said.

In a parallel universe, maybe.

"More like shrink wrap," I said, trying to make a pun.

She smiled uncertainly. "I don't get it."

"Neither do I," I said.

We smiled at each other for a moment, uncertain what else to say.

I decided to be honest. "I'm hoping people will pay me to gather information for them and give them reports."

Karen's face lit up. "I had a roommate in college who did that. She wrote people's term papers for them. She made *tons* of money."

"That's my goal," I said. "Money by the ton."

Already I was thinking the office lease probably would turn out to be a complete waste of money.

After Karen left, I stood at my new, empty desk and looked out the front window at the view of the almost-empty parking. For some reason, the previous PI had not left behind his chair. After a few moments, I leaned against my new, empty filing cabinet.

To my memory, in all of the mystery fiction I had reviewed over the years, no detective had ever done these two acts.

Karen suddenly opened the front door and ducked as she entered. She was dragging a rolling office chair. "The aroma therapist who used to be in D221 left this behind. It still has a rather strong floral scent."

It was also a bit wobbly. But it enabled me to sit down at my detective desk. It would do. It absolutely would do.

"Thanks!" I said. "Can I bring you a taco when I come back from lunch?"

Karen smiled. "That's sweet. But no. I have some wheatgrass and sprouts in my office."

How exactly does that differ from eating fresh lawn clippings? I wondered, now in full detective mode.

She ducked again, gracefully, as she departed, and I watched her click across the parking lot toward the leasing office.

In my first official act as an unlicensed private detective with a furnished office, I stepped out my front door, locked it and started my lunch hour.

I picked up a few pens and notepads at Office Depot and grabbed my laptop computer from my apartment. Then I hit the Taco Bell drive-through and headed back to my office.

I liked the sound of that. *Heading back to my office.*

In crime novels, the private eye often spends a lot of time just sitting at his desk, drinking whiskey, reading newspapers, cleaning his gun and waiting for a new client to wander in, lured there by desperation and his tough-guy reputation.

I had no reputation, of course, and no gun. I couldn't legally advertise. Nor could I legally investigate. I also had no entrepreneurial experience. But, other than that, I was now in private business, and I was set up to investigate...research...something.

TWENTY-SIX

It didn't take long for the first *something* to happen.

Someone who looked like a client barged in while I was finishing my second taco and surfing the web at my detective desk.

He was a big guy, much bigger and heavier than me. I knew immediately that I could take him – in a fifty-yard foot race.

"Where is he?" he said, talking fast and looking wild-eyed. "Where's that son of a bitch who calls himself a P.I.?"

I glanced at his tight-fitting sports coat, looking for the telltale bulge of a gun in a shoulder holster. Beneath his coat, he appeared to be one big bulge. *Fat? Muscle?* I couldn't tell which. And I didn't want to have to find out.

"The one who *used* to have this office?" I said helpfully.

"I gave him a thousand-dollar retainer last week to follow my ex-wife. Where's my report? I want my money back."

Instantly, I had a stroke of detective genius. "Maybe I can help you find him." It seemed a better choice than letting Big Guy stuff me into the middle drawer of my filing cabinet.

"Are you an investigator?"

"Somewhat," I said, being completely honest.

"How are you gonna find him?"

"Him" turned out to be somebody named Lazarus Popkin.

I felt the stars immediately line up in my favor. Not many P.I.'s on planet Earth would have that name.

"I'll check my contacts, make some calls, shake a few trees," I said. "Come back in a couple of hours."

Using Google, it took me about three minutes locate Lazarus Popkin's new whereabouts. He now had a private mail box in Corpus Christi. And a Skype phone number. And he was calling himself an "investment investigator."

You can run, Lazarus. But you can't hide. Not from the long arm of... the World Wide Web.

After exactly two hours, Big Guy was back. "Okay, where is he?"

I tore off the top page of a new legal notepad. "Here's his info."

Big Guy glared at it. Suddenly he smiled.

"Corpus Christi. I know all kinds of people in Corpus. I hope Lazarus can swim."

He folded the notepad sheet and stuffed it into his shirt pocket. "How much I owe you?"

I hadn't given that any thought. I picked a number out of thin air.

He seemed incredulous. "Fifteen dollars? That's it?"

Obviously, I needed to work harder on my pricing scheme.

"It's the move-in special, today only," I said. "Tomorrow my prices go up. Way up."

He pulled a twenty out of his very cash-thick wallet and tossed the crisp bill onto my desk.

"Keep the change," he said.

After he left, I thought about framing the twenty, or maybe getting change for it and framing just the first dollar.

Twenty bucks was just enough to buy Joan and me some dinner at Kerby Lane Café. Especially if we both had hamburgers.

I decided I would spend it all.

After I took care of business first.

I was eager ready to stamp "Solved" on Case 001 and put it in my filing cabinet. But I still needed to order the self-inking rubber stamp. And I had forgotten to buy file folders at Office Depot.

I hadn't kept the case information, either. It was now in Big Guy's shirt pocket. And I had failed to ask for, and write down, his – my first client's – name and contact information. Even Sherlock Holmes had to rely on referrals and repeat customers to stay in business.

But, clever detective that I am, I suddenly remembered an old trick from my past. *It's elementary school, my dear Watson.*

I took a freshly sharpened pencil and rubbed the side of the lead against what was now the seemingly blank top sheet of the legal pad. Lazarus Popkin's address and phone number dimly reappeared in the shallow indentations.

Suddenly and amazingly, two lost clues had been recovered.

Of course, I could have just gone back on Google, used the history feature and found him in seconds. But I didn't yet have a printer in the office.

The sheet from the legal pad contained the only actual case notes I could file.

I hand-printed "SOLVED" across the top.

Businesswise, I would have to do better, much better, when – or if – I had Case 002.

TWENTY-SEVEN

"You need more protein," Joan said.

We had fallen asleep after we made love, and I had missed my midnight snack. Now it was dawn. As I struggled to untangle from the covers and sit up, Joan handed me a plate of crackers neatly arrayed with triangular little wedges of ham and cheese.

She looked terrific. And terrifically awake. She had showered and dried her hair. Now she was wearing my robe and sipping from a mug of coffee.

"That's your answer to everything, isn't it?" I said as I yawned. "Protein."

"You're welcome," she said.

She stuffed a freshly layered cracker into my mouth. "Protein, sex and shopping."

"In that order?" It sounded like *"Imf hat odor?"* as I chewed.

"At the same time might be nice," she said.

A cup of hot tea was on my bedside table, another wakeup gift from Joan. I took a sip. She had cooled it down just right with a little bit of milk and sweetened it with some honey.

I watched her as she dressed quickly, real estate formal this time. Dark pantyhose, dark skirt, white blouse, dark blazer and heels. We each kept small collections of work and casual clothes in our respective closets, a logistical necessity. She checked her makeup and was ready to leave before I finished the tea and plate of food.

"I have a showing in a half hour," she said. "Then I'm meeting Samantha for lunch. I have a hair appointment at two, and after that, I'm going by Nordstrom's to look at shoes for the little boys, and then I'll stop by Central Market to get us some fresh salmon and green beans for dinner. What will *you* be doing?"

"Investigating. Researching. Studying," I said, chewing. "Being a two-fisted man of action."

"Well, you *were* quite a man of action last night," she said, smiling. "Don't forget to make up the bed."

She kissed me and strode out the door, clearly ready to corner the Austin real estate market. Or at least sell a house or two.

She always insisted that I make up the bed. At her house, I always did. At my apartment, I always did *not*. Not immediately, at least.

I would be at her place tonight. So I would have all day today *and* tomorrow to make up my bed before she came over again.

After she went out the front door and locked it, I contemplated getting up. To go anywhere with an investigation, I would first need to get out of bed. And I would need many more clues.

I thought about this while I finished off the crackers, cheese and ham.

She was right as usual: I *did* need more protein. Already, I was thinking a bit more clearly.

A few minutes later, I deduced that I needed to rest up a bit from the exertion of chewing. I put the plate on the bedside table, fluffed my pillow and quickly drifted off to sleep again.

At first, I dreamed I was a small child again, playing with plastic boats in my bathtub. The bathwater seemed big enough to be a small lake. The little boats moved long, straight distances when I pushed them. But one after the other, the boats sank. Freud or Jung no doubt would have something to say about that. I didn't ask myself how I would know that at age four.

But the dream soon evolved. Now I was at the murder scene again. Or what I thought was a murder scene. The Austin cops were still convinced it was suicide, and they were sticking to that conclusion. Their case was closed, they insisted. Yet they continued investigating, poking around in the grass and bushes that surrounded the body, looking for something.

"What are we trying to find?" I kept asking the cops as we searched. For some reason, they were letting me help them, and we were moving as a group through the park.

"Clues," Sgt. Marklin said, over and over. "We're looking for clues. Useful clues."

Mr. Granola was there, and so was the Swagman. "Find some clues," they kept saying.

Suddenly, the dead woman sat up and got to her feet. "This is stupid," she said. "You're all clueless." She brushed the dirt and grass off her clothes and gently touched the bullet wound in her forehead.

"Let me know if you figure out how I died."

Then she walked away and was gone. But the police and I kept looking, looking.

And Mr. Granola and the Swagman kept intoning, "Find some clues. Find some clues. *Find* some clues."

I woke up, sweating and tangled again in the sheets and bedspread.

Somehow, someway, I *will* find some clues, I vowed to myself as I carefully made up my bed.

TWENTY-EIGHT

It was just a hunch, nothing more. That's what I tried to make myself think.

But it *was* something more. In truth, I was still troubled by the "clues" dream.

I drove to the running trail that paralleled Lamar Boulevard, parked my car and started walking.

The late-afternoon temperature was hovering right at simmer, and the air smelled and tasted dusty and dry. But the trail was alive with earnest, sweaty runners, some striding alongside dogs panting on leashes.

I was the only human in sight *not* wearing at least five-hundred dollars' worth of logo-emblazoned athletic gear.

I moved along the trail, staying several paces to the right of it, so I wouldn't get trampled by the young, the restless and the impossibly fit.

The spot of the murder had been cleaned up and now was hard to find. But finally I recognized it and stood in the inadequate shade of a young tree while I looked down at the grass and dried leaves.

What did I expect to find? The cops and CSIs had checked the area with care and expertise. Could a recent graduate of the Advanced Online School of

Private Investigation turn up something they had not seen?

I stared at the spot where I had found the body and moved outward fifteen paces, carefully looking down at the ground. Then I paced back to the murder spot and moved outward again.

In my mind, at least, I was creating the spokes of a well-searched circle.

I had no idea if experienced investigators actually did this. Murder-scene search techniques had not been covered in my coursework.

Fifteen minutes later, I realized my mind and body were both wandering. I was thinking about making love to Joan, and I had lost count on an outward spoke. I was pushing through some bushes well outside the search circle.

My shoe came down on a dry leaf, and I sensed something hard beneath it as my sole pushed against the dusty-soft ground. It felt like a small stick or a slender stone. I stopped, crouched down and carefully moved the crushed leaf aside.

I thought at first that I had found a pink cigarette lighter. But as I brushed the dust from around it, I realized I had found something better. Something that might be full of clues: a USB-port flash drive.

My first instinct was to be a good citizen and call Sgt. Marklin.

My second instinct, however, was much stronger. I wanted to help Sgt. Marklin avoid wasting time and taxpayer money. I could do that first performing a little research. I could consider, ponder, study, examine, check out – but not illegally *investigate* – what I had just found. It might have nothing to do with the dead woman, and, if I could determine that, I would save the City of Austin some money. If it *had* belonged to the dead woman, it might be full of clues to her identity and the reason for her death.

I dug the flash drive out of the dirt and held it in my hand like a prize. Then my detective training kicked in: *Fingerprints, doofus!* My whorls and friction ridges now were all over the drive. If it had belonged to the dead woman and she had been murdered, I had just made myself a very prime suspect.

Exhibit A, your honor. A flash drive that belonged to the murder victim. We found the fingerprints of the defendant, Erwin Tennyson, all over it.

I pocketed the flash drive quickly and walked toward the parking lot feeling like a thief. Every few steps, I looked over my shoulders to see if anyone was noticing me.

The scattered runners on the path seemed focused only on striding, looking cool, getting buff and not falling victim to heat stroke.

Was the Swagman watching me from back in the trees? Even the homeless had weapons, sometimes.

What if the dead woman had been killed because of what was on the flash drive? Had she somehow managed to throw it into the bushes just before she was shot?

Had someone pursued her, shot her, took every identifying item off her body and accidentally dropped the flash drive while making his – or her – escape?

I reached my car and climbed in, feeling the flash drive in my jeans pocket pressing against my leg. And feeling as if I had somehow just put my life in danger.

The Sunfire seemed to sense my urgency. It started on the first try.

I pulled out onto Lamar and headed north, staying just under the speed limit and watching for police cars or any sign I was being followed.

Case 002 was in my pocket. I realized that now. I hadn't wanted to admit it to myself. But the mystery of the woman's death was the main reason why I had taken the detective course and leased the office.

I looked at my watch. Almost five o'clock. Time to meet Joan.

I wanted to drive to my office and drop off the flash drive. But there wasn't time, and I wanted to keep its location secret a bit longer until…until…what? Until I had more supplies and furnishings?

Until I had a loaded gun in the top drawer?

All the way to my apartment, I wished I had enrolled in the Advanced Online School of Accounting.

Or Plumbing. Or Ancient Greek History.

Or even Refrigeration Repair.

TWENTY-NINE

I spotted Joan's well-waxed Infiniti the moment I pulled into my apartment building's parking lot. And I detected dinner being cooked even before I unlocked my door. *Basil…onions…garlic…*

Instantly, I felt safer. I settled into a better mood.

"Hi, honey, I'm home!" I called out cheerfully as I entered.

"Cute…but not funny," Joan said, keeping her eyes on her stovetop multitasking.

A big pot of spaghetti was boiling and she was carefully adding browned ground beef to a smaller pot of simmering spaghetti sauce.

I walked over, kissed the back of her neck and nuzzled her hair.

"Smells delicious," I said.

"Me or the sauce?" she asked, stirring saucily.

I gave her another neck kiss and slipped my hands beneath her red apron. "You *and* the sauce."

She set down her stirring spoon, turned and gave me a stirring embrace. One hand slid down and pushed deep into one of my back pockets.

"Ooo, it's caught," she said. She pretended to try to pull it out. But mostly she just kept palming one cheek of my butt. It was one of her favorite games. Mine, too.

An hour later, we made very satisfying love on full stomachs and quickly fell asleep.

When I awoke just before 9 p.m., Joan was picking up our clothes from the floor and pitching them into our laundry baskets.

She always did laundry in a very meticulous manner, checking pants pockets and turning the pants inside out to minimize wear on their visible surfaces.

Right away, she found the pink flash drive in my blue jeans.

"What's this?"

It was not quite the same thing as finding lipstick on my collar. But I knew Joan well enough to recognize a sharp tone of suspicion. I could tell she was thinking: *Are you having an affair with some chippie who likes hot-pink flash drives?*

My mother initially had tried to give me a high-minded middle name: *Probitas*, Latin for "honesty." Erwin *Probitas* Tennyson. And my father, fortunately, had convinced her that it – or any other middle moniker – likely would just get me beaten up on schoolyards. So I had grown up without even a Harry S Truman empty initial.

But there had been no shortage of maternal reminders that I must always tell the truth. My mother loathed liars. Probably she still did, twenty years in her grave. Indeed, her first husband had been a liar, a cheat *and* a scoundrel. He had left her penniless and pregnant with my older sister and taken off with a small-town beauty pageant runner-up half his age.

I sat up in bed and told Joan exactly where and how I had found the flash drive and why I was now worried about fingerprints.

Joan repositioned the flash drive between her thumb and forefinger and stared at it.

"So now *I'm* the prime suspect," she said. "I just covered your fingerprints with mine."

I climbed out of bed. Usually, when I did this, Joan leered a bit at my nakedness and smiled. But this time, she just kept looking at the hot-pink drive.

"It may not have anything to do with the case," I said.

"Or it might have *everything* to do with it," she said.

She took the flash drive into the bathroom and pulled a small bottle of rubbing alcohol and two cotton balls from the cabinet.

I didn't need to ask her what she was doing. She swabbed and rubbed every surface. Then she carefully wrapped a facial tissue around the drive and picked it up.

"That should take care of our fingerprints," she said.

"And any others that were on it," I said, unhelpfully.

She pushed past me, took the flash drive over to my PC and plugged it in.

Windows XP did not recognize the drive's format.

"So it's nothing," I said.

Joan again ignored me. Still naked, she pulled the pink device out of the USB port. She lifted her Macintosh laptop out of her briefcase and opened it up.

I went back into the bedroom and pulled on my sleeping shorts. I didn't like standing around with nothing on but the FM radio.

The Mac booted up. When Joan plugged in the flash drive, its directory showed just one file, *luno_es.doc*.

"Open it up," I said.

Joan was one step ahead of me.

The file popped open. Some kind of document. I squinted at its first sentence.

"La malgranda hela suno rozo de malantaux monto."

It appeared to be something in Spanish or Portuguese, with a bit of French mixed in. A book? A dissertation? The document was 329 pages long, according to *Word*.

It wasn't a clue to murder. I felt certain of that.

But I figured it might be murder to read.

THIRTY

The next day, I sat at my private detective desk and stared again at the hot-pink flash drive. It was lying on the desktop in a small plastic bag.

Something about it still bothered me, but what?

Was the game afoot? Or was I merely stubbing my toes against wild imaginings and unfounded suspicions?

My desk still had none of the classic furnishings of a noir gumshoe. This bothered me, too. The top drawer still lacked a pint bottle of bourbon or gin and some kind of gun, maybe a quickly grabbed .25 or snub-nosed .38. But I hated booze, and Joan – when I finally told her about the office – had declared firmly that there would be no guns going off, accidentally or on purpose.

She was, however, at least a marginal fan of British detective novels. After a stern lecture on how I was wasting my retirement money, she had apologized and presented me with a six-pack of V8 juice and a loaded water gun to keep in the top drawer. In return, I had solemnly promised her: *"I won't squirt until I see the whites of their eyes."*

I drummed my fingers on my detective desk for a while, and then I decided it was time to move from safe detecting to safe citizenship.

I opened a lower drawer, found a pair of a pair of latex gloves and carefully pulled them on. Then I got a small manila envelope from my desk and addressed it to the Austin Police Department's lost-and-found department. I assumed they had one. I carefully printed a bogus return address on the envelope's upper left corner, pulled the flash drive from the plastic bag and dropped it into the mailer. I also enclosed an anonymous note: "Found this near Lamar Blvd., in a park."

The envelope had a self-adhesive flap, so I didn't have to worry about licking it and leaving behind my DNA.

I glued three stamps to the envelope, carefully locked my office door and walked to a mailbox a half mile away.

It would be picked up at 5:30 p.m., according to the posted schedule.

I dropped the envelope in.

Maybe the flash drive had been stolen and tossed aside, and not merely lost by a jogger. In that case, it might get returned to its rightful owner.

It felt good to be rid of it. I walked back to my office, combining exercise and crime-fighting with every stride.

Erwin Tennyson, healthy AND solid citizen.

The late-morning sun felt warm on my back.

As I unlocked my office door again and stepped back inside, I suddenly figured out what had bothered me about the drive. One of the strange-looking words in the document's opening sentence – *malantaux*-- had kept floating around in my consciousness. But I still had not taken the time to look it up.

I had taken no French in high school or college. Yet something about the word looked wrong as I typed it into Google. Did I remember its correct spelling?

I did. Google popped up a small flood of results in a foreign language I could not read. But about twenty entries down, I saw an English summary with *malantaux* defined as "behind" in Esperanto.

I thought Esperanto had joined the pantheon of dead languages several decades ago. Clearly, I was very much *malantaux* the times. The search results revealed Esperanto still was very much alive, a veritable vampire of strange verbs, adverbs, nouns and pronouns seemingly sucked from other tongues. I scrolled through several dozen links, all of them posted in Esperanto, and all of them containing *malantaux*.

I wondered how much it would cost to get the document translated into English. Maybe I could hire a student at UT-Austin to do it cheaply. Maybe Amazon or Half-Price Books had a used and really cheap Esperanto-English dictionary.

Suddenly, I remembered a saying from the current vernacular.

Maybe there's an app for that.

There was.

I found and downloaded a freeware Esperanto-to-English translator program and opened it up.

That's when I discovered I had *not* kept a copy of the *luno_es.doc* file on my laptop.

I called Joan.

"I figured you would forget," she said. She was at her house, using her computer to update a property listing. She emailed the file. "You should have it soon. Bye."

I opened *Windows Explorer*, but now I didn't have a Wi-Fi connection. The business complex's "free" system suddenly was down, and all of the other Wi-Fi signals in range were encrypted.

I called Karen.

"The technician says he'll be over first thing Thursday morning," she said.

It was Tuesday afternoon.

I left my detective office and drove my dirty blue detective Sunfire to my favorite Starbucks. Someone was sitting at my favorite detective table, drinking a latte and posting tweets on Twitter. Indeed, all other tables were taken, as well. So I sat in the middle of a couch, between a college student who was studying advanced economics and an old guy who was soundly sleeping while holding the *Wall Street Journal*.

I saved the attached file, opened it, started the Esperanto-to-English program in a separate window and performed a copy-and-paste of the first sentence into the translation box: *"La malgranda hela suno rozo de malantaux monto."*

The translation appeared almost instantly in a separate box: "The small bright star rose from behind a mountain."

The freeware program also had the option to translate a full document. All I had to do was log onto a website and pay $29.95 to unlock the feature.

I decided, instead, that I would just copy and paste one sentence at a time into the translator. Then I would move the results into a new Word document and keep repeating the process.

Fifteen minutes later, I was halfway through the first page. But someone had vacated a table that had a power plug beside it. I moved to the table, plugged in, got online again and charged the $29.95 to my battered MasterCard.

The translation program revealed that the *luno_es.doc* file indeed *was* somebody's novel manuscript. The title page and author's name were missing. But I could tell right away that it was a science-fiction fantasy tome.

The same vapid shit that's now keeping Frank Arkandale rich, I sneered to myself.

I opened a separate WordPad screen and typed a few notes as I scanned the novel's first few pages. A character named Parchko, exiled leader of the Twelfth Moon of Quarktune, was in love with Quarktune's queen, who was being held hostage on the Seventh

Moon. (No doubt of Quarktune.) And she would not be released unless the Six-Dimensional Sword of Urrgham was given over to somebody named Mogbar, who wanted to marry the queen against her wishes and…Zzzzz.

I had been right the first time. The book *would* be murder to read.

In English *or* in Esperanto.

THIRTY-ONE

Had I caught a red herring? Or had the red herring caught me?

It was mid-afternoon now. I closed my office early, not that anyone cared, and drove south on Lamar Boulevard, passing fast-food restaurants, struggling small businesses, the Texas Department of Public Safety headquarters, Half-Priced Books and the Quadrangle, a large complex with restaurants and shops on the ground floor and apartments above.

It was a warm day. People of all ages were out walking their dogs, jogging, riding bicycles or dining beneath canopies and patio umbrellas.

As I waited at a stoplight, watching them, I realized now how much I missed working in newsrooms. I couldn't think and focus effectively unless I had the sounds and motions of people moving around me.

Just past the stoplight at 45th and Lamar, I made a right turn into Starbucks. The three-o'clock crowd was now thinning out. But a few souls were still scattered about at the tables, jabbing their fingers at iPhones or typing on iPads and laptops.

I got my usual drink and sat at my usual table. I started up my laptop and hunkered down to think.

The great fictional detectives, particularly, Poirot and Holmes, seemed to have uncanny knacks for observing and remembering tiny, easily overlooked details. Later, they used those details to build ironclad, logical frameworks that trapped killers.

My brain, unfortunately, was a constant swirl of disassociated images and unrelated detail: my locker combination in junior high school (32-0-32); the wingspan of a P-51 Mustang (37 feet); the capitol of Vermont (Montpelier); the library return date (September 7) for *Secrets of Success in Private Investigation*; Joan's birthday (November 8); the fact that I still haven't replaced the missing middle button on my favorite corduroy shirt (maroon); how one dateless summer semester in college I was so bored that I spent most of each day playing pinball machines; the time in the Navy near North Vietnam when I took a picture of a Russian freighter passing at close range and saw a Russian sailor taking a picture of my ship – he gave me a small wave, and I returned it; the impatient looks on the faces of the restless runners as they waited for Sgt. Marklin to reopen the jogging trail. I had watched *them*, appalled and fascinated at their monomaniacal focus on just moving head. Meanwhile, I had paid almost no attention to the vital minutia of the death scene.

Focus, damn it! I said to myself. *Remember! Dig it out!* The grass was green; the leaves partially covering the body mostly were brown, but some were green. *Were they green?* Now I wasn't sure.

Maybe I wasn't sure of anything anymore.

I opened the translated Esperanto document again and scrolled through it. And again, I saw nothing in it that held my interest. I wanted now to delete it and move on; my finger lightly pressed against the DEL key. But just as I decided to push it, I decided to wait and call Joan first. I wanted her to know what was in the file. I wanted to be sure I wasn't about to make yet another rookie detective mistake.

When I reached her, she was driving to her final showing of the afternoon, a duplex on Braker Lane. It was outside her usual sales territory and at least two notches below her preferred price and commission range. But she was doing what she could to keep adapting to the Great Recession's deep and lingering real estate crisis.

"I've taken that file off my hard drive," she said. "Save it if you think you'll need it. I have absolutely *no* interest in swords and sandals in space."

"Neither do I," I said. But after I hung up, I did *not* press the DEL key. Instead, I moved the document into a new folder that I cleverly and presumptively named "Murder."

After that, I sat for a while and just watched people come in, get their lattes, frappuccinos and mochas and go, talking of Michelangelo.

If I had a Dr. John Watson writing on my behalf, he might now be describing how I appeared to be completely lost in thought, my mind no doubt racing through great quantities of facts, news reports, scientific formulas and astute observations about the attire, actions and attributes of those around me.

In truth, my head finally was focused on just one general concept. My office rent was due in two days, and thus far, I had made just twenty bucks – and spent at least thirty times that much – trying to be a private eye.

Just as I neared the bottom of my drink, Joan called again.

"The client was a no-show. So we're going to Philadelphia for the weekend."

"You and the client?" I said.

"You and me, Erwin. I've booked us a flight on Southwest. We're leaving Austin tomorrow morning at ten-thirty, and we'll be in Philly by late afternoon. We're staying in a hotel next door to a five-star restaurant at the edge of Old Town. You'll be two blocks from Benjamin Franklin's grave."

"Philadelphia?" I said. "I've never been there."

"That's why we're going. Neither have I."

"Just like that?"

"Just like that. It's how I roll," she said. "You should know that by now."

I did know. Yet her spontaneity still kept catching me by surprise. To keep up, I could no longer fall behind on doing my laundry, getting my suit dry cleaned or keeping my refrigerator stocked with things to cook.

With Joan, I had to be ready – and available – for almost anything.

THIRTY-TWO

A light, warm mist fell as Joan and I stood in the northeast corner of Christ Church Burial Ground and huddled beneath her umbrella.

Barely twenty feet away from us, trucks and cars flowed past noisily on Arch Street, while other vehicles waited for the traffic lights to change at the 5th Street intersection.

"People believe it's good luck to leave a penny on Benjamin Franklin's grave," Joan said. She was looking at a small map and brochure describing the graveyard's 1,300 historic markers, many of them dating back to the American Revolution.

Some visitors to the cemetery obviously were hoping for something better than mere good luck. They had violated Franklin's famous dictum that "A penny saved is a penny earned." Nickels, dimes and even a few quarters were mixed in with the pennies scattered across his worn flat marble slab. "His grave makes about three thousand dollars a year," Joan said.

It didn't take me long to do the math. More than two hundred and twenty years after his demise, Ben Franklin's moldy bones were still making money – infinitely more than I was making as a detective. I was burning through my retirement savings faster than a speeding bullet.

We walked on to look at some of the other markers. Four other signers of the Declaration of Independence also were buried here, along with Revolutionary War heroes, early government officials, prominent Philadelphia merchants and politicians, and even the man who had made the cemetery's iron gates.

But there was something uniformly sad about the historic site. And it wasn't the grey light, nor the growing dampness.

Most of the headstones – even the ones of people revered in American history --were dissolving with age, and many of their inscriptions no longer could be read. Some three thousand people buried in the cemetery no longer had markers at all and were now completely lost to time.

When we came to the small headstone for John Taylor, Christ Church's gravedigger for fifty years, I thought of the dead woman back in Austin, her body zipped up in a plastic bag and stuffed in a refrigerated locker in the Travis County morgue. If no clues to her identity emerged soon, she would end up in a pauper's grave marked only with a number on a small piece of metal. And someday, her anonymous burial site might be ploughed over and covered with the asphalt for space 538 of a Wal-Mart parking lot. She, too, would be lost to time.

Yet why did I care? Earth's soil already had absorbed billions of unremembered people, all the way back to the earliest humans. *Dust to dust.*

"Why are you so quiet tonight?" Joan said.

After the graveyard tour, we had gone back to the hotel and made love. Now we were having dinner in a seafood restaurant on Market Street.

"Sorry. Just thinking," I said.

I was eating an appetizer cup of New England-style clam chowder and waiting for an order of boiled shrimp over ice.

Joan was having a Manhattan and a shrimp cocktail and waiting for a half-dozen fresh oysters on the half shell, Malpeques from Prince Edwards Island.

"Thinking about what?" Joan said.

"Thinking about you."

Joan smiled. "Liar. I'm trying to take you away from that murder case for a while. But I'm not succeeding, am I?"

I reached across the table and took her hand. "Most of the time, you are. Yes." I meant it.

"But?"

"The graveyard visit clarified my thinking a bit."

"And what did the great detective conclude?"

I reached across the table again, this time with my fork, and stabbed one of the shrimp in her cocktail.

"I've concluded," I said, gesturing with the shrimp, "that I have no bloody idea what the hell I'm doing."

"So, what's your new plan?" Joan said. "Plumbing? Ancient Greek history?"

"I've been banging my head against a wall," I said, wagging the fork harder. "When we get back, I'll start banging my head against the other side of the wall."

I made one banging gesture too many. The shrimp suddenly popped off the tines, somersaulted past Joan's head, left a little splat of cocktail sauce on the brick wall beside our table and dropped out of sight behind the table cloth.

"That's my Erwin," Joan said, demurely.

She reached across the table with her napkin and wiped a little sauce speck from my left cheek.

"Tilting at windmills with a fork instead of a lance."

THIRTY-THREE

The morning after we returned from Philadelphia, I drove to my office with new resolve.

Be the detective. Solve something today, I told myself.

It sounded good.

Maybe, I mused as I waited for a stoplight to change, *I'll record a CD of motivational sayings. Pearls of wisdom and witty gems that would help new private investigators overcome their early-career self-doubts.*

Straight from the Fertile Mind and Files of Erwin Tennyson, Private…uh…

There would be *no* market, I realized, for motivational CDs aimed at private *researchers*.

Two minutes after I sat down at my detective desk and wondered what to do first, a matronly woman came in. Well-dressed, late sixties, her gray-and-white hair freshly washed and styled.

"Are you the private investigator?" she said.

I took an extra second to answer. Was she an undercover cop looking to bust unlicensed private detectives? Was Sgt. Marklin hiding just outside the door, handcuffs ready?

"I'm Erwin Tennyson, private *researcher*," I said. I carefully emphasized all three syllables of the final word. There would be *no* doubt on the recording if she were wearing a wire.

"I'm Karen's mother," she said, offering her hand. "Margaret Cullingham."

I relaxed, took her hand, shook it gently and smiled. "Karen's a gem," I said. "She's the best leasing agent I've ever had."

It was the truth, even if she was the *only* leasing agent I had ever had.

I expected Margaret Cullingham to break into a proud, motherly smile and thank me. Instead, she just scowled.

"I wanted her to go to Julliard or Harvard Medical School. Or even the law school at the Sorbonne. Somewhere that she could meet a substantial man," she said. "But no, she insisted she had to follow her own star."

"So what did she do?" I said.

"She got an associate's degree in real estate at Austin Community College. And now she's managing this...place." There was no hiding the disdain and disappointment in her voice.

"Well, she does a really good job, and she's a lot of fun," I said, trying to cheer her up. "How can I help you?"

Janet sat down in my rickety client's chair, a recent two-dollar purchase at a garage sale, and unfolded a legal-sized sheet of paper showing the photocopied outline of an urban lot. She set it on my desk and carefully turned it around so I could read its labels.

"I need to you investigate this lot. I am thinking of buying it. It's about a mile from here."

"Investigate it in what way?" I said cautiously. I pictured myself having to go to some dingy city office, stand in a long line and ask to see copies of plats, deeds, tax liens, mineral-rights records and other paperwork that Joan might understand but I would not. Already, I was dreading this case.

Janet got a very serious look on her face. "I need you to measure the lot and make sure I will get exactly what I pay for."

"Measure the lot?" I said. "That's it?"

"Yes, to the inch. To the half inch. I want you to verify that none of the three neighbors' fences have encroached."

I realized I still had not figured out an hourly rate to quote to clients. Would she balk at thirty bucks? I could borrow Joan's 35-foot Stanley FaxMax tape measure, poke a stick in the ground to hold the far end in place and stretch it across the longest part of the lot in four hops.

"My rate…" I said.

She held up a hand and cut me off before I could get out: *"…is thirty dollars an hour."*

"I can pay you four hundred dollars," she said. "It shouldn't take you more than an hour or so. But I expect very, very careful measurements, down to the half inch."

I barely heard that. Four hundred bucks would pay my office rent, with a sawbuck left over for a nice lunch.

"Let me check my assignment book," I said.

I opened my new desk journal and tilted it up carefully so she couldn't see its unmarked pages. Then I pretended to peruse a long list of entries.

"I had cancellation this morning," I said, trying not to sound like a dental office manager. "I can do it."

She insisted on paying me in advance, and I did *not* say "That's okay, I'll just bill you."

After she left, I eyed her check carefully, looking for any flaw that might cause it to be refused by the bank. It looked as good as gold. Maybe *better* than gold.

I called Joan. She was, for the moment, working at home, in her real estate office.

"Emergency," I said. "I need your help."

"For one of your investigations?"

"Yes."

"No," she said."

"No?"

"No."

"Why not?"

"Because."

"Because why?"

"Because you know *why*, Erwin Tennyson."

"I do?"

"Yes, you do."

"You don't want me to be a detective. Is that it?"

"I sell real estate. I don't have time to play private eye. That's your game."

"Well," I said, thinking fast, "can you help me with a tricky real estate matter?"

"Possibly," Joan said.

"It's very complicated, and I really need your expertise."

"Flattery," Joan said, "will get you nowhere. Or, it can get you everywhere. It all depends."

"I need to borrow your thirty-foot tape measure for a few minutes."

"That's it?"

"Yes."

"Maybe," Joan said. "And--?"

"And what?"

"With you, Erwin, there's always some kind of string attached. What is it this time?"

"It's a matter of mind *and* body," I said, trying to sound suave and persuasive.

"In other words, it's prurient. Okay, I'm listening." she said.

"Could you hold one end of the tape measure while I stretch it out?"

Joan laughed. "It's not *that* long." She laughed again and kept laughing until she made herself cough. Finally, she caught her breath. "Sorry, Erwin, I couldn't resist. I've been reading contracts all morning. What are you measuring?"

"A vacant lot in Hyde Park."

"You're buying a *lot*? With *what* money?"

"A client," I said carefully, "is having me investigate a lot she is thinking of buying. She has given me a copy of the plat and wants me to verify its dimensions. All I have is a one-foot ruler."

"Sometimes, that's all you need," Joan said.

THIRTY-FOUR

She met me at the lot a half hour later and gave me a kiss as she climbed out of her Infiniti.

I had feared the suburban plot would have rough mounds and shallow mud holes and be overgrown with high grass, weeds, old tires and other flotsam. But it was flat and freshly mowed. Its "Lot for Sale" sign appeared almost brand new.

"I did a little research for you," Joan said as we stood on the sidewalk. "It used to have a house, one story, pier-and-beam foundation. The house burned down in 1932. Nothing since then. A neighbor bought the lot after the fire and had it cleaned it up so his kids and other kids could play on it. It stayed in that family and passed from father to son to grandson. The grandson lost his job recently. He wanted to will it to his kids, but he has decided he needs the money."

I looked at her, feeling amazed. "How did you figure all of this out while you were driving?"

"Deep secrets of the trade," she said, holding up her cell phone. "I looked up the listing and called the seller's agent. She and I are old friends."

The ground felt firm under my shoes. But the stiletto heels of Joan's Jimmy Choos kept punching into the soil as we walked to the first spot where we would measure the lot's width.

"This is going to cost you dinner," Joan said.

"How about tacos to go?" I said. "I'll have ten bucks left after I pay my office rent."

"Okay." She extracted another heel from the mire and grimaced as she looked down. "And maybe some new Choos."

"Next case," I said. "I promise I'll help buy you some new" – I pretended to sneeze – "ah-ah-ah Choos."

"Cute, but not funny," Joan said.

She smirked, pushed the end of the real estate tape measure against a neighbor's fence post and handed me the reel.

"Okay, start walking," she said. She tried to keep her shoes from sinking by the stern as I stepped across the lot, walking backward.

When the tape ended, I squatted down and made the thirty-foot mark in the grass.

Joan let go of her end. I reeled it in. She tiptoed across to me, took the end again and squatted down to hold it against the mark. Her nice knees were revealed as her skirt slid up and her four-inch heels knifed at least an inch into the ground.

I pulled the reel out to its end again and made another thirty-foot mark in the dirt.

"Measure…for Measure," I said, emoting like a bad actor as I stood up.

We repeated the reel-in, squat-down, sink-at-the-heels and reel-out process.

This time, as Joan tugged at her skirt, she caught me looking.

"There are better ways, Cassio, to see my knees," Joan said, demurely.

"Aye, my lady," I said, emoting again as I backed up, unspooling tape. "And what ho, even nobler ways to seize them and hold."

"Cute but *not* funny," Joan said.

"By the way, my friends call me Cassio-nova." I smiled at my cleverness as I backed into the other neighbor's fence.

"Just shut up and measure," Joan said as her heels sank again. "For measure."

I touched the tape to the post that held up a section of aging cedar pickets. "Sixty-seven feet, ten and three-quarter inches," I said, triumphant. "It's an inch wider than the plat indicates. That's exactly what the client wants to know."

"Write it down," Joan said.

I did. I pulled my detective notebook from my shirt pocket, drew a little rectangle and noted the width across the bottom of the box.

"Okay," Joan said. "Now we'll measure across the middle and the far end. Then we'll repeat the process along both edges and across the middle to verify the depth of the lot." authoritatively.

"Roger that," I said.

"And later," she said, looking down now at her heels, "we'll discuss your contribution toward my new Jimmy Choos."

"Those heels have been doing a mighty fine job of aerating the soil," I said.

Joan stared at me and frowned.

"My contribution toward new Jimmy Choos," I said, nodding most agreeably now. "Yes, ma'am. Roger that, too."

As we finished the final measurements, I suddenly remembered something I had witnessed at the park, at the Jane Doe death scene.

One of the crime scene investigators briefly had pulled out a small tape measure and used it to compute the distance between two points in the grass. Footprints? Blood stains?

I had not watched him closely enough to observe or recall. I had been too distracted by the faces and movements of the investigators stoically working around the deceased. And I had locked in on Mister Granola, the Swagman and the small mob of impatient humanity jogging in place just outside the crime-scene tape.

The all-important fine details that Holmes and Poirot used to crack cases had completely and utterly escaped me.

I felt somewhat sure that the grass beneath the CSI's tape measure had been brown. Yet, despite the dry August heat, it could have been green. Or yellow. Or yellow-green. Or yellow-brown. Or--?

I knew just one thing for certain. My name and photograph would *not* be added soon to the Advanced Online School of Private Investigation's "Distinguished Alumni" web page.

THIRTY-FIVE

At my detective office, I typed up a short "Private Researcher's Report." I truly wanted to head it "Private Investigator's Report." But that one-word difference could mean a fine and possibly some jail time if it fell into the wrong hands. So my "Researcher's Report" gave Margaret Cullingham the exact dimensions, down to the half inch as instructed. It also informed her that the lot was exactly 102.5 square feet bigger than the latest plat indicated.

Joan graciously had helped me figure this out, right after she carefully cleaned the dirt from her heels and pronounced the Jimmy Choos "still somewhat serviceable." She had pulled out her crisp, new, silver, solar-powered real estate calculator embossed with "Joan Larkin" and demonstrated each step necessary to convert the lot's extra inch of width and two extra inches of depth into square feet.

"This is basic math, Erwin," she had said as the answer popped up. "I can't believe you didn't learn this in junior high school."

"That was *fifty* years ago," I had said in self-defense. "And never once, in any book review, have I needed to calculate square feet."

I emailed my report and got Margaret Cullingham's reply in minutes: "Great work! Thank you! Next time I buy another lot, I'll definitely hire you to investigate it!"

I printed out her message and pulled out a fresh file folder. I was ready to label the folder "CASE 003," stamp it "SOLVED" and put the case notes into my filing cabinet. But measuring a lot had not really been an "investigation" worthy of a detective. The only mystery had been determining if I could actually handle and read a tape measure.

I started a to-do list and wrote "Order 'Case Solved' rubber stamp" at the top. I couldn't think of anything else to add to it, so I put it aside. As I did, I moved a piece of paper and found two other small to-do lists beneath it.

Both of them had just one unfinished task: "Order 'Case Solved' rubber stamp."

I really need a secretary, I thought as I wadded them all up and threw them away.

Actually, I first needed to solve a case that would bring in enough money to pay for the rubber stamp.

Then I would need to stamp a lot of cases "Solved." Only after that could I hire a secretary, so *she* could stamp and file the future case folders.

I leaned back in my chair, stared out at the half-empty parking lot and daydreamed about what the secretary might look like. Blonde? Brunette? Redhead? Well-attired, of course, in the latest business fashions, except on Casual Friday, when tight sweaters and equally tight blue jeans could be the uniform of the day.

Karen strode across the parking lot, leading a short, rotund, bald-headed man away from one of the available office spaces. She towered above him by more than a foot, and he seemed to be looking directly at her ass as he tried to keep pace, taking one and a half steps to her one.

My secretary will not be basketball-tall, I vowed. I wanted someone I could face eye-to-eye without having to stand up.

Momentarily, I pictured Joan as my secretary, smiling sweetly as she set a cup of hot cocoa in front of me. "Now," she would say, tapping a well-manicured finger against the daily planner on my desk. "It's time for you to get off your cute butt and do some actual work. Your first task today is to order that 'Case Solved' rubber stamp."

A few minutes later, the front door to my detective office suddenly opened. Karen ducked in and smiled.

"Thanks for helping Mom with the lot," she said, gesturing with her cell phone. "She just called and said she bought it."

I returned her smile and gave her my best "Case Solved" look. At that point, I could have just said "You're welcome!" And, if I had, it might have been a sunny day forever for Erwin Tennyson, Private Researcher.

Instead, I blurted out the obvious. "You and your mother could have measured that lot yourselves and saved a bunch of money."

Joan, had she been present, likely would have clamped her hand over my mouth before I could finish. Then, later, she would have lectured me sternly on the perils of going into business without any inklings of Business 101.

But she was not present, and now I wished she was.

Karen frowned. Until now, I had never seen her frown. She sat down in my client chair and slumped forward a bit so we were facing somewhat eye to eye.

"She's richer than God, Mister Tennyson," she said, looking hurt. "She often spends money just to have something to do."

I held my tongue, almost literally. I rested my chin in my hand and clamped my cheeks a little tighter than necessary.

"She *never* buys vacant lots, but I talked her into at least thinking about buying the one in Hyde Park. I told her your office rent was due, and I didn't think you were making enough money to cover it. So we created a job for you." Tears formed in Karen's eyes. "I try really hard, Mister Tennyson, to take care of my clients."

"Call me Erwin," I said, sincerely meaning it. "You do a wonderful job."

I wanted to offer her a Kleenex, but I had not yet added a box to my detective desk. How had I overlooked this important detail? In virtually every private detective novel I had reviewed, the male clients typically looked grim, almost shell-shocked, as they told their story. And the female clients almost always burst into tears and needed a Kleenex.

I tried to offer Karen a Post-It Note to catch her tears. But she just shook her head and pressed a sleeve to her face. She was wearing a black pantsuit over a white blouse that was only slightly frilly. The tears left two tiny, barely visible damp spots on her sleeve.

"Your rent is due by five o'clock today. The office closes promptly at five," Karen said, suddenly all business again.

"Do you have change for a twenty?"

She nodded.

I pulled out my wallet. I had cashed her mother's check on the way back to the office. The twenty crisp Jacksons momentarily had provided a pleasant little bulge, heft and aroma in my pocket.

She pulled a ten out of her purse and handed it to me.

Easy come, easy go, as they say in the great detective novels.

She also pulled out a small pad and wrote out a receipt.

"Thanks, Karen, I really mean it," I said.

"You're welcome, Mister Tennyson." She got up to leave.

"Call me Erwin, please."

"Goodbye," she said. "Have a rockin' day."

She went out the door and I watched her walk across the parking lot toward the leasing office.

I realized I was still holding the Post-It Note, and words were scribbled on it: "1. Order 'Case Solved" rubber stamp."

I added "2. Get Kleenex," and stuck it to one of the few remaining visible spots on my desktop.

Despite the warm, bright sunshine outside, now I felt glum. But the feeling didn't last. My cell phone suddenly beeped. Text message. Big Paul wanted me to meet him for drinks. "ASAP," he added. "Urgent."

"On my way," I texted him back.

Is the game at last afoot? I wondered as I locked my detective door and climbed into my detective car.

Or did Big Paul just want to show me his manuscript and con me into trying to help him get it to a publisher – after I bought him coffee and a croissant?

THIRTY-SIX

Something was afoot. I sensed that the moment I strode into Starbucks.

Big Paul had commandeered my favorite table. And he had an iced tea lemonade already waiting for me.

He had even gotten it in the huge new cup that was one ounce south of a quart.

He also had upgraded his wardrobe. Instead of his usual Hawaiian shirt, cargo shorts and leather sandals, he was now wearing a tan, summer-weight blazer, a pressed blue-denim shirt, clean, rancher-style blue jeans, rattlesnake-skin cowboy boots and his Texas Ranger Stetson.

"Two Splendas, right?" He slid the big cup toward me as I sat down.

I nodded. "Thanks!"

"I was down at the cop shop," he said. That explained his improved attire.

He took a short sip of his coffee. "Little Paul saw an inquiry from an embassy yesterday. The El Salvadorian – is that how you say it?"

"Salvadoran."

I had been to San Salvador once, twenty three years ago, on a reporting assignment shortly before I became a full-time book reviewer. The story had involved a crop disease in produce exported to Texas from El

Salvador. Some kind of green bean. There had been fear the disease would get exported, too.

"Salve whatever," Big Paul said. This time, he took a bigger sip of his coffee, apparently impervious to its near-boiling temperature. "One of their citizens hasn't been heard from in a while, and her parents are worried. All they know is, she's somewhere in the United States."

"That narrows it down a bit."

Big Paul ignored me. "Little Paul says she kinda-sorta fits the description they sent out. About the right age and height as the vic. He's asked for a DNA sample. It may take a while."

"Not much to work with," I said.

"It gets better. Her parents live in an isolated village. No phone and no computer access."

"Is Little Paul asking me for some help?"

Big Paul gave me a sly little smile. "He let me write down her name while he wasn't looking." He unfolded a small scrap of paper and slid it across the table to me.

"Marisol Alfaro," the note said.

"He doesn't actually want to know if you can do any Google searches. But if you happen to do some – purely as a citizen volunteer *researcher*, of course – I might accidentally blurt out something about what you learn. And he may accidentally overhear what I blurt."

"Of course," I said. "Accidentally." *Erwin Tennyson, King of the Pro Bono Private Eyes.*

"Little Paul's real busy with a multiple gangbanger homicide that went down last night. So if you accidentally come up with something, he's hoping you'll accidentally let me know what it is, so I can accidentally tell him over coffee soon."

"Accidentally on purpose, of course."

"It's the only way, Erwin. Otherwise, he'll have to arrest you for being an unlicensed private detective."

"*Researcher*," I corrected him. "I'm a private researcher. There's no law against gathering information and trying to put it together."

Big Paul grinned and took another drink of coffee. "Yep, that's right," he said.

"What will *you* be doing to help solve the – *his* – case?" I said.

"Managing my retirement portfolio. Writing my novel," he said.

We're not exactly Spenser and Hawk, I thought.

"But if you need to share some of your quote-unquote" – he made little squiggly marks in the air with this fingers – "research with Little Paul, I'll see if I can work him into my busy schedule and maybe leave some information on his desk."

"Accidentally, of course."

"Oh, absolutely," Big Paul said. "Accidentally."

THIRTY-SEVEN

I went back to my office, sat down at my desk and tried to work hard at being an unlicensed private investigator.

I desperately needed a Dr. Watson right now. But Big Paul would not fill that role. And Joan, as usual, was busy doing her Joan things.

Think, Tennyson, think, I thought.

Nothing immediately came to mind. But Karen, the basketball-tall leasing agent, walked across the parking lot with gazelle gracefulness. I watched her for a while. She was leading a potential office client, a short, fat, red-faced guy in his forties. In her heels, she towered over him by almost two feet. He was balding already and moved like he was ready to launch a bookkeeping business. Or die of an early heart attack.

Suddenly I remembered a trick I had once seen in a book about how to build plots in a novel or a screenplay.

I took out an almost-fresh legal pad , drew a small oval near the center of its top sheet and wrote "Marisol Alfaro, El Salvador woman in Austin" inside the oval.

Around the edge of the oval, I drew several little lines extending outward in all directions.

Why might a young woman from El Salvador end up dead near a yuppie running trail in Austin, Texas?

Had she been a drug mule? I wrote "drug mule?" at the end of one of the lines.

Had she been an illegal immigrant working as a prostitute? I picked another line and jotted "illegal immigrant/prostitute?" at its end.

Was she a Salvadoran undercover cop working a case? That seemed impossible, but the book had stressed writing down anything that came to mind, no matter how absurd it might be. I wrote down "undercover cop?"

Other lines got labels: "businesswoman?"; "journalist?"; "diplomat?"; "agriculture expert?"

Somehow, she didn't seem to fit a "college student?" label, but I stuck to the rules. I did the same with "Salvadoran astronaut?" and "somebody's undocumented housekeeper?"

After a while, I watched Karen march back across the parking lot, leading her client toward her office. That seemed a good sign for her. If he made it to her desk without dropping dead, he might lease one of the many available spaces that flanked mine.

They walked into her office, and I returned to the intricacies of my investigation.

Immediately, more possibilities popped up. And they became more and more absurd: "Salvadoran comedienne (somebody didn't like her act)?"; "Salvadoran singer/musician?" – Austin was renowned for its live music; "Salvadoran looking for work as a movie extra?"; "Salvadoran bike racer?"

I ended the process with "here to open a Salvadoran restaurant in Austin?" and "Salvadoran Mafia?"

I looked out my window for a few moments and watched a Toyota Land Cruiser cruise through the parking lot like a smooth-moving rhinoceros. It dwarfed my Sunfire. But I felt smug in the knowledge that I got much better gas mileage and my car was paid for.

I picked up the legal pad, rested my chin on a fist and carefully pondered what I had.

Nothing.

Absolutely nothing.

I tore off the sheet, wadded it up tightly and lofted a trash can shot for two points.

It arced softly, hit the rim…

Tennyson scores!

…and bounced off onto the floor.

THIRTY-EIGHT

Once I yielded to the times and opened Google again, I quickly figured out that "Marisol Alfaro" likely was El Salvador's "Sally Smith" or "Jane Jones." Hundreds of hits popped up.

The next thing I discovered was that my Spanish completely and totally sucked.

But, great detective that I am, I soon deduced that I could click on the "Translate" tool and use it to transform Salvadoran web pages into serviceable English.

After two hours of reading translated Tweets, MySpace pages and company and school websites, I rubbed my eyes and concluded that I now had no clue what to do next.

So I folded up my laptop, clicked off my office lights, locked my detective door and drove home.

Sherlock Holmes had his violin. Hercule Piorot had his fixation on fastidiousness and trying to keep precisely 444 pounds, 4 shillings, and 4 pence in his bank account.

Maybe I would just grab a random book, take it out on my balcony, sit in my white plastic chair and read until sunset.

Once I opened my front door, I knew I had no idea where to randomly grab.

My apartment's bookshelves were tight with books. I also had books stuffed horizontally on top of the book rows and books arranged in several small stacks on the floor.

Periodically, Joan goaded me into selling off a few bags of old paperbacks and hardbacks at a used book stores or donating some of my overabundance to a homeless shelter.

Still, I had hundreds of left-over review books in my home office, and I was always a sucker for buying 25-cent books from bookstore bargain tables and at neighborhood garage sales.

I needed more shelves. But my apartment had no more furniture space.

I closed my eyes, stuck out my hand and pulled out the first book I touched: *The Return of Sherlock Holmes*.

I stuffed it back into its slot. *To hell with detectives for a while*, I thought. *Pick something lighter-hearted.*

I closed my eyes, stuck out my hand again and grabbed another book – a ragged paperback I could tell by its feel. I carried it out onto my balcony and didn't look at it until I sat down.

It was John Bunyan's *The Pilgrim's Progress*.

I tossed it over the balcony railing, heard it plop two stories below, and just sat in my chair for a while. I leaned back with my hands behind my head and watched the sun drop closer to the trees.

After an hour, I walked downstairs, retrieved the book from the sidewalk, brought it back upstairs and squeezed it into its space.

Joan arrived her night at my apartment. A real estate investor suddenly had rescheduled his appointment with her, so she had picked up some hamburgers.

"You don't need more bookshelves," she told me as we ate at my small table. "You need *fewer* books."

"Books are my life," I said. "What if I woke up in the middle of the night, trying to remember a scene from *Wuthering Heights*?"

"Three things," she said. "Why would you do that and why would you even care?"

"That's two things."

"Wait for me to finish."

"Okay."

"Are you waiting?"

"Yes."

"Get a Kindle. Sell your books," she said. "That will give you more room on your shelves. In fact, we could get rid of some of these book cases and replace them with floor lamps, some wall hangings and big potted plants here, here and here."

"I can't write in a *jungle*!" I said.

"Sure you can. You write at Starbucks. That's the human jungle. I bet you even write in that ugly little office."

"How do you know it's ugly? You've never seen it."

"Don't need to," she said. She leaned across my small table and gave me a kiss. "At this point in our relationship, Erwin Tennyson, I am intimately familiar with Austin real estate *and* with your interior decorating skills, specifically the lack thereof."

"Speaking of intimacy," I said.

She put a finger to my lips and smiled at me.

"Finish your hamburger first."

THIRTY-NINE

The next morning, Joan had no early appointments. And I had no appointments whatsoever. So we slept until 8 a.m.

I woke up first and pulled on grey T-shirt over my black sleeping shorts. I went into the kitchen, poured myself a bowl of Cheerios and wet them down with vanilla soy milk. I peeled a banana and was using my spoon to cut it into pieces when Joan came into the kitchen and caught me.

"That's why God invented knives," she said, still squinting the sleep out of her eyes. She had, however, carefully combed her hair before leaving the bedroom. She was wearing a floral silk pajama bottom and – in honor of the continuing summer heat – nothing else.

"Good morning," I said, gazing more at her nice breasts than at her stifled yawn. "I thought Benjamin Franklin invented knives. He invented almost everything else in America."

"He didn't invent last night."

There was a nice little bounce to her bosom as she pulled her favorite bowl down from my kitchen cabinet, poured in some instant oatmeal and water and slid the bowl into the microwave.

While her breakfast cooked, I opened my apartment's front door, retrieved the *Austin American-Statesman* and sat down with it at my bowl of

Cheerios. There were two big headlines. The Republican-dominated Texas Legislature was proposing massive budget cuts for schools, health care, and welfare programs. And Idaho Joe's Beer & Barbecue Emporium, supposedly an "East Austin institution since 1947," had burned to the ground last night.

"Lovely," I said, as Joan sat down across from me. She saw where I was staring. She grabbed the newspaper's entertainment section and held it strategically while she took her first bite of oatmeal.

Sometimes, Joan could be shy even when she was being brazen.

For a few minutes, we read and ate our breakfast in silence.

I got another good glimpse when we traded newspaper sections. Now she was reading Business and I was reading the comics.

Finally, as she finished her oatmeal, she tossed down the Business section and smiled at me. This time, she didn't seem to mind that my eyes kept shifting up and down.

She could be brazen, sometimes, when she was being brazen.

"Tonight, at my place, I'll have a little surprise for you," she said.

"From Frederick's or Victoria's?" I said.

She blushed slightly. But her eyes sparkled. "Wait and see."

"I love suspense," I said. "And I love costume dramas."

"I know," she said, smirking. "Especially the ones that involve lingerie."

"You feed those fantasies. Rather frequently and willingly, I might add."

"I don't want you to forget about me or lose interest," she said, blushing again slightly.

"I'm having more sex than five guys my age. And it's the best sex ever. How could I lose interest?"

Joan smiled, leaned across the table and gave me a kiss.

"Yes, it is the best sex ever for me, too," she said. "But I also love you for your mind."

"Even when I do crazy things like try to become a detective?" I said, trying to sound both funny and hopeful.

"There are challenges in every relationship," she said. Her tone suddenly was noncommittal. She saw my look of disappointment. "Time to go to work."

Joan dressed in her real-estate power clothes, kissed me again and left to go to a title company. One of her clients had sold a small house in a small Texas town, and the closing documents needed to be signed and faxed by 10 a.m.

My pocket planner had nothing in it for today. Nor for the rest of the week, month or year.

So anything's possible, I thought. *Something could happen.*

Or nothing.

I tried to push that doubt out of my mind as I walked to my clothes closet and pulled it open.

Dress for success. Make something happen.

When he first went into the printing business in Philadelphia, Benjamin Franklin – the great inventor of stoves and American police patrols – found that he could make things happen just by faking industry *and* prosperity. When he had no printing jobs in house, he put on his good work clothes and carried big rolls of paper through Philadelphia's streets. The idea was to at least *appear* to be doing something – and doing it well – so people would notice, remember and solicit his bid the next time they needed printing.

It worked for B. Franklin. It could work for me.

But how exactly could an unlicensed private detective appear busy enough and prosperous enough to attract "research" clients?

I could put on good clothes and carry around …what? A chip on my shoulder? A Humphrey Bogart expression on my face? A clipboard?

I pulled out a white business shirt, a dark-blue silk tie with tiny grey diamond patterns, and my long-neglected black business suit. The suit had a few visible closet wrinkles, and it definitely needed to be dry-cleaned. But what the hell.

People would notice, I was sure.

FORTY

Big Paul noticed.

"Who died?" he said.

He took a sip of his coffee and sat down at my table.

I had spent part of the morning sitting alone in my detective office. But no one had dropped in and noticed my changed attire, nor my charged-up entrepreneurial spirit. So after thirty minutes of drumming my fingers on my detective desktop, I had driven south to 44th & Lamar and taken the last remaining table in the crowded Starbucks.

"No one died. I just felt like dressing up a bit today," I said.

Big Paul had changed his look, too. He was once again back in his retired Texas Ranger attire, this time a blue, white and yellow Hawaiian shirt, faded olive-drab cargo shorts and flip-flops. He looked vaguely like a small-town Minnesota banker or Iowa accountant ready to spend a day on the beach at South Padre Island.

"Business must be good if you're wearing a suit," Big Paul said.

"That's the idea," I said. "Hum a few bars and fake it."

He took another drink of coffee. Then he got up and walked over to the cream container, added a small amount and returned to his chair.

"Little Paul let me see something else yesterday. Purely by accident, of course," he said.

"Can I accidentally see it, too?"

Big Paul smirked. He pulled a small piece of paper from his shirt pocket, unfold it and set it in front of me. He turned it so I could read the words.

"Graduate teaching asst., U. of El Salvador. Native novelists."

"Native novelists?" I said.

"Little Paul's trying to get her picture from the university. But the school's closed for a while. It's between semesters, and there's some kind of national holiday or teachers' strike or revolution going on."

Two clues quickly and solidly clicked into place. The flash drive probably *had* belonged to the dead woman. And there was now a good possibility she *was* – or had been --Marisol Alfaro.

I realized I had just reached the dividing line between private researcher and private eye. *Unlicensed* private eye.

I could call up Sgt. Marklin right now, tell him what I knew and suspected, and let him take the case from there. But, once I did that, he might say I had withheld important evidence – specifically the flash drive and the novel file – and hindered his investigation. He could have me in handcuffs and headed for the Austin city jail five minutes after I hung up the phone.

Still, I decided I would take the chance. I could tell Big Paul what I had turned up and how it might be connected. I could emphasize that I had found the flash drive several days after the young woman's death. And I had been a good citizen and mailed it to the police, not realizing what I had. Then – just slightly lying through my teeth – I could say that I had not sensed any connection at all between the Esperanto file and the missing Salvadoran woman, until now. The cops then could take it from there, and I could move on to investigating – to *researching* – something else. Maybe a lost-dog case. Or trying to track down somebody's missing yard gnome.

But just as I opened my mouth to confess, Big Paul got a text message, quickly flipped open his phone and grimaced as he read it

"Gotta run," he said. He got up from the table and tossed his empty coffee cup into the trash can near our table. "The wife says we're out of milk, bread, eggs and leeks. So I'm off to Randall's."

His flip-flops popped against the bottoms of his feet as he strode to the front door.

Just before he stepped out, however, he looked back at me and grinned. "A retired Texas Ranger's work is *never* done."

I smiled and gave him a little wave goodbye.

My work, I sensed, suddenly was just beginning.

Like it or not – and I did not like it – I would have to learn more in a hurry about swords and sandals in space. *And* their connection to El Salvador.

Frank Arkandale, I'm sure, would be willing to tell me everything he knew, as well as why he was God's gift to the genre. He might even say something that would help lead me to Marisol Alfaro's killer. *If* he didn't bore me to death first.

FORTY-ONE

"I'm in L.A.," Frank said when I called him. "I'm signing a movie deal and talking with a few network executives about a possible TV series."

"Wow, congratulations."

Frank tended to acknowledge good wishes by seemingly ignoring them. "Get us some Shiner beer, Er, and come out to the hacienda Thursday night, about seven," he said.

It was Tuesday afternoon, so I had plenty of time to burn and no actual desire to spending it reading paperbacks about swords and sandals in outer space.

I called Joan to see what she was up to.

"I was just about to call you," she said. "My good friend Amy Northton wants me to come up to Chicago for a couple of days so we can go shopping on Michigan Avenue. We're planning to hit every block of the Magnificent Mile."

"Can I go, too?" I knew the answer even as I said it.

"Amy's husband will be at a dental conference, so it's girls' day out. Sorry. But maybe, if you're good, I'll bring you pizza slice. Or a garter belt."

"Make it both," I said. "I'll miss you."

""I'll miss you, too. But there *is* a consolation prize," Joan said. "I've moved my appointments to next week, and my flight leaves Austin tonight at eight. So I have a few hours free, *after* you buy me lunch."

We rendezvoused at our favorite Thai-Chinese restaurant on Lamar Boulevard, not far from state police headquarters and the Half-Price Book Store.

I ordered my usual chicken fried rice, with fork. No chopsticks.

Joan never had a "usual" anywhere we ate. She always found something different to try, even at small-menu restaurants we had visited many times before.

"Gang garee gai," she said to the trim, beautiful Thai waitress, who spoke only fair English with a high, singsong voice. No doubt an illegal immigrant.

"Gangrene what?" I said as the waitress left.

The waitress's trim little backside undulated as she walked quickly toward the kitchen. I had not listened carefully enough to Joan's order, of course. I had been doing what I imagined most male private investigators typically did in this situation: idly speculating on what the waitress might be like in the sack. Not that I would ever find out.

"Gang *garee* gai." Joan corrected me sharply, catching my eyes and clearly not amused. "Chicken in a yellow curry with carrots, potatoes and bell peppers. It's made with coconut milk."

I was still watching the waitress out of the corner of my eye, trying to hone my increasingly subtle surveillance skills. "Sounds delicious," I said.

The gang garee gai or the girl?" Joan had watched my eyes. She was smirking now.

"The gang garee girl," I said earnestly. "I mean the gai. The girl garee gai."

"You're hopeless, Erwin Tennyson," Joan said, laughing. "And a completely hapless liar."

"But you still love me."

"Yes. Of course, I do."

"Why?"

"Am I being interrogated now? Is this an investigation?"

"Yes. And I'm plying you with eggrolls."

She reached across the table and took my hand. "I love you because you – unlike others in my past – are always exactly who you say you are."

"You mean I'm not a master of disguises?"

"You're just a big old Boy Scout, always watching out for me, always bringing me flowers, opening doors for me and telling me I'm pretty."

"Well, you are."

"And," she paused for dramatic effect. "I really like holding onto your cute little butt when we make love."

"Ah ha," I said. "The truth comes out."

Joan smiled. "Do I need to get you a big magnifying glass and a deerstalker hat? Or can you just see that I'm crazy about you, you big goof?"

I reached out and took Joan's hand across the table. I leaned over, kissed it gallantly and held her gaze. "I love you, too, my lovely house lady," I said.

Joan chuckled. "You make me sound like some kind of kept woman."

"Well, 'my lovely house lady' sounds a bit more chivalrous than 'my lovely Realtor,' don't you think?

The trim little waitress brought our food, and this time I gave her nothing more than a slight, peripheral glance. I continued holding Joan's lovely hand, and I gently lifted her arm a bit, so the waitress could table Joan's gang garee and my chicken fried rice.

"Enjoy!" the waitress said as she left.

"I do," I said, not breaking my lock on Joan's eyes. "And I will."

"Yes, we will," Joan said, smiling demurely as we loosened our love grip and reached for our eating utensils.

We still had four hours to eat – and play – before I had to drive her to the American Airlines gate at Austin-Bergstrom International Airport.

FORTY-TWO

The next morning, I slept late, left my bed unmade and ate and spooned my Cheerios and soy milk out of a beer mug. While I read the *Austin American-Statesman*, I wondered if Joan and her friend Amy already were on block two of Chicago's Magnificent Mile.

There was not much good news on the front page. Another "Austin legend" café had burned down, and this time arson was suspected. The restaurant recently had failed its monthly health inspection and gotten closed for a week.

Frank and I had known each other for many years, but he had never been over to any of my apartments. Actually, I was happy about this. Pre-Joan, I had been a terrible housekeeper. And I didn't want Frank to discover that I owned only a few of his books and had not completely read any of them.

Fantasy and science fiction, frankly, were not my Klein bottle of tea. I had tried to care, but I cared not a whit for Maldort, the combat-weary leader of Clan Calipham on the planet Ectopia, even if tens of thousands of Frank's readers did.

On the other hand, I could *see* myself inside Phillip Marlowe's ratty car, driving. I could *feel* the cool metal of a little .25 tucked inside my coat pocket as I got ready to save a fallen damsel from the big sleep.

I could even make my mouth twist into a reasonable facsimile of a film noir frown. I had practiced it a few times in front of the little bathroom mirror in my apartment and the much bigger master bathroom mirror in Joan's house.

I could *not* see myself inside Prince Maldort's light red skin, raising a double-bladed *rachdama* – apparently some sort of sword that could slice through atoms and molecules – as I prepared to lead another *banzai* charge against the evil, green slimeballs that were trying to conquer his beloved Ectopia.

Just nuke 'em already! I wanted to scream. *Set phasers to annihilate!*

But, of course, Maldort couldn't do that, because his lover and queen, Albyanka, had just gotten herself kidnapped by the Grokomen, the green slimeballs, for the 500th – or was it now the 501st? – time.

Whenever Frank made bragging references to how a snarky reviewer for *The New Yorker* or the *New York Review of Books* had praised a particular passage on page 172 or 203, I just nodded my head sagely and said, "Yep, that grabbed my attention, too, Frank. Brilliant writing."

I had been always busy *not* completely reading the books I was paid to review. So, while I now had a nice collection of Frank's books on my shelf, I could not tell anyone anything about what was inside most of them. Dutifully, however, I always bought and had him autograph each new one that came out, and I told him I thought it was great. Then I smiled and nodded while he casually dropped the names of famous directors and producers who had called to congratulate him and mention possible movie deals.

How the hell does he do it? I wondered.

It was time, I decided, to actually read one of Frank's books. Perhaps even all the way through.

I stood at my book shelves and pondered titles for a few moments. Finally, I pulled out one of the last of his standard, Earth-based Westerns. *Cimarron Revenge* was the concluding paperback in his U.S. Marshal Wilson Grey series.

I took the book and a beer out on my balcony, sat in my chair and flipped through some of the pages. The afternoon was quiet, and the early September air was just cool enough to hint at fall.

There was nothing amazing or mysterious about any of Frank's sentences.

Articles, nouns, pronouns, verbs, adverbs, prepositional phrases, conjunctions and interjections.

All of the parts of speech, in various orders of presentation.

Wilson quietly slid off his horse and pulled his carbine from its saddle holster. The Hardeman Gang, he knew, would not expect him to attack from the rear...

After a few pages, I grew bored with Marshal Grey and his guns that almost never missed. I set the book down beside my beer bottle and just stared at the horizon for a while.

Maybe Frank was right, I mused. Perhaps I *should* just make up a bunch of stuff and try to write a detective story.

Or a science fiction novel.

High Noon on Neptune, whatever *it* was about, definitely was helping preserve his status as a multimillionaire.

Could I string together 200 manuscript pages, get them published, and be deliriously happy if I was lucky enough to make twenty or thirty thousand bucks from the book?

Hell, yes, I could be happy. Particularly with the money.

But first, physically and mentally typing 60,000 turgid words rife with swords and sandals might be like trying to climb Mount Everest with a refrigerator strapped to my back.

Why try?

FORTY-THREE

Thursday. 7 p.m.

I showed up at Frank's hacienda precisely on time. And once again I was the gullible geek bearing gifts of Shiner beer.

"Come on in, Er," he said when he opened his front door. His cell phone was pressed to one ear. "I'm talking to DreamWorks. Make yourself at home."

Frank usually had a housekeeper, a matronly woman old enough to be his twin sister. She kept his house spotless, but he sent her home every day at 4:30 PM and apparently lived and worked alone in his big house.

Now and then, especially around the time of the Golden Globe awards, the Screen Actors Guild Awards or the Academy Awards, Frank showed up in *People,* in entertainment magazines and on movie-star websites, in the company of well-known women at least half his age.

For as long as I had known him after he became famous, Frank seemed – at least in the tabloids   to be involved with a different woman almost every month. And the pairings frequently seemed blatantly structured for mutual publicity. A starlet or singer still on the way up or in danger of fading after a box office or album bomb could get an important, if temporary, boost by being seen with the famous Frank Arkandale.

169

Meanwhile, Frank's book sales got some bumps when fans of the actress or singer wondered what she saw in him and what he wrote.

Frank had apartments in Manhattan, Los Angeles, Miami and Vail, and I assumed those were his love nests. Austin, however, was his writing sanctuary. I had never met – nor seen any evidence of – his romances of convenience and market share at his ranch.

I sat at the kitchen table and pulled two cold bottles from the six-pack. I sipped slowly at my beer and listened while Frank kept talking in his home office. I could also hear him opening and closing filing drawers.

"The last time *The Killer from Cimarron* was optioned," I heard Frank say, "Paramount paid me sixty thousand, for six months. I can let you have it for a year for a hundred-K. That's a bargain these days for a Frank Arkandale book.

There was a brief pause. Then Frank continued talking. "I appreciate your situation, but I have a long track record of success and an image to protect."

Finally, Frank ended the call. "Okay, Sanders, nice hearing from you again. If you improve your position, give me a call." He shut his cell phone – "Hollywood asshole!" – grabbed a beer and sat down at the table. "How's your novel going?" he said to me.

"I haven't started it yet," I said.

Frank scowled. "So you're still playing at being a detective?"

"Yes. But now I'm not playing."

"You're scared, aren't you? You still don't think you can write a book."

"That's right," I said. Honesty, after all, had *almost* been my middle name.

"Listen to me, Er. Listen to me very carefully." Frank seemed almost eager tonight to get back into mentor mode. "Private detectives are a dime – hell, they're a *centavo* a dozen. Good writers are not. Don't waste your time, talent and experience on foolishness."

"I wouldn't know where to start," I said. Again, it was the truth. I had given some thought to the notion of a novel.

"Trust me on this one," Frank said. "A dead woman in a park is no story. Readers won't care. Publishers definitely won't care."

"But I care," I said.

Frank took a long pull from his bottle. "So use the movie approach. First we meet your detective character while he is on Case A. He has just concluded that the unidentified woman in the park killed herself, so that case is over. That's your page one. Suddenly he gets a call to investigate Case B. And it looks at first like just another drug deal gone bad. But your detective keeps digging and soon finds it's something big, really big. It reaches deep into the federal government or the military or the FBI or the CIA or the military-industrial complex. Your Austin private detective ends up chasing spies or terrorists or rogue generals through the *arrondissements* and sewers of Paris."

"I thin*k* the dead woman in the park is – was – from El Salvador. I want to help find out how she died. I want her parents to know."

"Noble. Very noble," Frank said. "And very dumb. Nobody will ever pay you a cent for it."

"I don't care," I said. "I'll figure some way to survive."

Frank picked up his beer and gave the dark-amber bottle a long stare.

"Maybe you will," he said finally. "Or, maybe you won't."

Thanks for your vote of confidence, Frank, I wanted to say. But I did not. Instead, I just picked up my beer bottle, too, and gave it an equally long – and stubborn – stare.

FORTY-FOUR

I drove to my office and was setting up my laptop computer when the postman entered bearing the morning mail, a single catalog.

"Is this yours?" he asked. He showed me the address label. He looked like an ex-professional football player. *Maybe a tackle or tight end?*

His hands were almost as wide as the catalog.

The label said "E. Tennyson, Pvt. Investrg." The catalog was full of the latest detective stuff from P-Eye Gear, the Wal-Mart of private-eye supplies. I was now on their mailing list, with a typo.

I nodded. "That's me."

"What do you invest in?" the postman asked. "I'm thinking of getting into gold."

I started to correct him. It would be easy to point out that the label was supposed to say "Investgr," for "Investigator," not "Investrg," for "investor-ing." But I suddenly realized he might not really be a postman. He could be an undercover Texas Ranger or state trooper looking to bust unlicensed private investigators.

Oh, a little of this, a little of that," I said, trying to appear and sound financial. "I'm just getting started."

"How do you feel about gold?" he said.

"Gold is good," I said, trying to think of something else more convincing to say. Then I remembered reading in the *American-Statesman*'s business pages that gold now was bringing record high prices. I had mentally kicked myself for not owning even an ounce of it, so I could sell it now and pocket the cash.

"But you want to buy low and sell high," I said, now remembering more of the article. "Real estate is beaten down, and so are a lot of stocks. Those might give you better returns if you can stay in for the long haul."

The postman nodded his huge head. "Good advice. Maybe I'll bring you my portfolio."

I nodded as he left but said nothing else. My mind now was full of dark thoughts, a nightmare of noir.

In Texas, the ex-Wild West, there now were laws and license requirements for financial advisors, too. Had I just violated the Texas Securities Act? Would the postman return later wearing a different uniform and slap cuffs on me?

Your honor, the defendant, Erwin Tennyson, was arrested after giving illegal investment counsel to an undercover officer, while said defendant also was working as an unlicensed private investigator.

"Mister Tennyson, how do you plead?"

"Guilty, your honor. Guilty and stupid."

I looked out my front door. The postman, if indeed he was that, was now climbing out of his delivery truck at the far end of the office complex. As he went inside another door, I locked up, got into my Sunfire and fled to Starbucks.

My timing was perfect. I got my favorite table and drank iced tea lemonade while I calmed down and looked through the P-Eye Gear catalog.

It had great stuff. Tiny camcorders. Devices to read deleted text messages. Bedside alarm clocks with surveillance cameras and voice-activated audio recorders hidden inside. Audio recorders that looked like flash drives. Electronic listening devices. Tiny GPS tracking devices that attach magnetically to vehicles. Covert digital video recorders inside pens, tie clips and flower pots.

Sadly, I had no equipment budget, and none of the cool gadgets could help me track down Marisol Alfaro's murderer.

I would have to do it the old-fashioned way.

With grit, determination and a lot of dumb luck.

FORTY-FIVE

At 45th Street, Burnet Road's four lanes funnel into Medical Parkway, a narrow canyon lined with medical clinics, doctors' and dentists' offices and miscellaneous small businesses. I decided not to go that way. I turned left, went past the Texas School for the Blind and took another left at Lamar, destination unknown.

After a few blocks of aimless driving, I knew needed to do something that resembled focused investigation.

I took a left on Anderson Lane and headed west. A few miles and detours later, I turned into the parking lot of Rich Garpmann's apartment complex.

Garpmann's car was gone. I pulled into an empty slot directly across the parking lot and watched his door in my rear-view mirror.

I knew a few things about him now. He often ran in the park where Marisol Alfaro's body had been found. That gave him the opportunity. And being a gun-club member and proud owner of a 1939 Gestapo-surplus Walther PPK pistol gave him the means. The Walther was the wrong caliber, of course. But if he owned one gun, he likely owned others. And he would not have wanted to toss his priced piece into Town Lake or have it buried in the city landfill after he killed someone.

Now I just needed to figure out his motive. I would be very surprised if it involved anything other than one of the classics of murder: sex, money or drugs.

Joan suddenly called my detective cell phone.

"What are you doing?" she said.

I kept my eyes firmly locked on the rearview mirror and Rich Garpmann's front door. And I used my free hand to shield my mouth and phone from prying eyes. "Stakeout," I said quietly.

"That's a great idea," Joan said.

"What is?"

"Steaks out. Taking me out for a steak."

I tried to keep my mind on Garpmann. But after three hours of sitting and watching cars and people come and go, I was tired, bored and hungry. And I desperately needed to pee.

"What will we do after steaks?" I said. The evening would still be young, and Joan likely would want to hit a mall before the stores closed.

"I thought we might go back to my house and play a game," Joan said.

She liked Monopoly, chess, dominoes and any board game her grandkids wanted to play. At best, I was mediocre at any and all of them.

My idea of a good game was emptying a bowl of popcorn while watching baseball, football, basketball or the Olympics on television.

"What kind of game?" I said, not hiding my apprehension.

"Oh, I don't know," Joan said, laughing and sounding coy. "Maybe pick a random page in the Kama Sutra and see if we can make it work?"

My mood brightened immediately, until I remembered the last time I had looked at the Kama Sutra. There were many contortions now somewhat beyond my capabilities to twist and bend.

"What if we can't…what if we pick something we *can't* make work?"

"There are *lots* of pages in the Kama Sutra," she said. "I'm sure we'll find something else."

My detective intuition told me Rich Garpmann would still be around tomorrow. And my Sunfire started right up, on the second try.

"On my way," I told her.

Rock beats scissors, and the Kama Sutra definitely beats tiddlywinks.

Every time.

FORTY-SIX

The next morning, I woke up vowing to be more like Mike Hammer and directly confront Rich Garpmann. So, I called his office and told the receptionist my name was Harold Hinkley. "Mr. Garpmann asked me to give him a call," I said, trying to give my voice an undertone of snarl.

"I'm sorry, Mister Hinkley," she said. "Mister Garpmann is no longer one of our employees."

"Why? What happened?"

"I'm sorry, sir. He's no longer with us. That's all I can say."

Had he quit? Been fired?

Was he dead?

I could have asked any of these questions, but I was flustered by the unexpected change. And I knew she would refuse to answer.

Think, Tennyson, think!

Somewhere in my detective course, there had been a paragraph describing an old investigator's trick, followed by a stern warning that it was now illegal

Pretexting. That was the term. *The act of tricking people into giving out information they are not supposed to reveal.*

"He loaned me a laptop computer a couple of weeks ago," I said, "and I need to return it. How can I reach him?"

It sounded lame even to me, but it *was* pretexting, and I was making a genuine effort to use it.

Pretexting had gotten an entire chapter in my detective course. The training manual had warned that using pretext to get telephone records or bank records was a federal crime. And then the lesson had covered various ways to get unspecified information using pretexting.

"I'm sorry, sir," the young woman said tersely. "I am *not* allowed to give out that information."

Clearly she had had some counter-pretexting training. She hung up.

I drove to Rich Garpmann's apartment complex, ready for another stakeout. Without a job, he would be spending more time at home, I reasoned.

He was *not* still around.

His car was gone from his parking space.

His curtains were pulled open and his apartment door was half open.

I got out of my car and walked up the stairs. I pretended I was looking for another apartment number as I strolled along the second-floor walkway.

As I passed Rich Garpmann's door, I stopped and looked.

Nothing was inside. Not even a scrap of paper on the floor.

Fresh vacuum cleaner marks were visible in the carpet.

Rich Garpmann was, in fact, gone. *Long* gone.

I was at a dead end. But as I drove back to my detective office, remembered one other lesson from my online training, in the skip tracing chapter.

"Send a letter—or even a blank sheet of paper-- to the skip's old address. Mark the envelope 'ADDRESS SERVICE REQUESTED.'"

I had a small package of envelopes and a book of stamps in my detective drawer. Joan had given them to me "just in case you decide to search for a job and need to send out your resume."

I folded a blank sheet of paper, slipped it into a #10 business envelope and mailed it to Rich Garpmann's old address.

A week later, the U.S. Postal Service returned my envelope with a yellow label attached.

Mister Granola had a new address in rural Oregon, nearly as far from any big city as possible. A post office box in a town of 200.

"Ah, ha," I said. It was a discovery worthy of sharing and debating with a Watson. But Joan was somewhere out in Round Rock or Pflugerville, showing a house. So I just said "Ah, ha" again, aloud to myself, and considered this new evidence as I sat at my detective desk.

I made a crime-fighter's fist and thumped it boldly against my desktop.

Fleeing the scene of the crime. I have you now, Mister Granola. That was my first thought.

My second thought was: *Get real.*

What's-His-Name Spenser could fly across the country and work a case for free for several weeks, just for the justice of it. That was the great thing about being a fictional P.I. Your bills magically got paid; your fight cuts and gunshot wounds miraculously healed; and, inevitably, when you blundered into an overload of trouble, Hawk and his sawed-off shotgun or Capt. Quirt and the Boston Police Department showed up just in time to save your butt.

Mr. Granola may well have just moved to the moon.

With one plane ticket or one U-Haul trailer, he had escaped the not-so-long arm of Erwin's Law.

Now I had to consider the possibility that Rich Garpmann was *not* the killer. Otherwise, I had no investigation. And the mystery of the woman's death might never be solved – if, indeed, it really *was* a mystery.

I opened my detective filing cabinet, dropped the envelope into the "Case 002" folder" and pushed the drawer shut with dramatic determination.

It was time to find and follow Suspect #2. The Swagman.

Tomorrow.

FORTY-SEVEN

I staked out the Lamar Boulevard running trail's parking lot just after dawn and listened to classical music inside my Sunfire.

At 7:00 a.m., the KMFA announcer said it was 79 degrees in Austin, with an expected high of 101 and just a 20 percent chance of scattered evening showers.

Two minutes later, in the midst of a short piano piece by Maurice Ravel, the Swagman came out of the woods for his morning panhandling. I watched him in my rearview mirror. He was overdressed for the early-fall heat, but his ragged clothes seemed surprisingly clean. He walked past my car, apparently oblivious to my mission, and headed toward a street corner about a block from the jogging trail.

He carried a neatly lettered cardboard sign. Part of it said "Please Help." I couldn't read the rest of it.

I waited until he reached a street corner near the park. When he unfolded his "Please Help" sign and started walking down a line of line of rush-hour cars waiting at the stoplight, I made my move.

In the Navy, I had learned absolutely nothing about advancing quietly through woods and underbrush. But I had seen enough war movies to know that I needed to move slowly, watch the ground for booby traps and keep eyeing the trees for snipers.

My bigger fear, however, was snakes. I didn't want to step on a sleeping rattlesnake or copperhead and get bitten. So mostly, I just watched the ground as I eased ahead. And I tried not to leap out of my skin each time a green or brown gecko suddenly darted in the leaves and skittered out of sight.

Fortunately, the Swagman's camp was barely two hundred feet off the running trail, in an area well camouflaged by thick underbrush and a stand of small trees. It seemed to consist only of a makeshift tent and a pile of rocks.

I looked back to be sure the Swagman wasn't coming. Then I moved closer.

The tent was a large piece of translucent plastic sheet draped over a pair of small tree limbs. Some of the branches had been broken off, so the thickest part of the limbs lay flat on the ground and flanked a grimy, worn sleeping bag. The ends of the tent were held down by rocks on each side, and the rear of the tent pressed up against the outside of a ten-foot-high wooden privacy fence that marked the end of the park and the start of someone's private property. Several million-dollar houses lined the hill above the park. But they could not be seen through the brush and trees. The rocks carefully piled about four feet from the front entrance of the tent formed a rough circle just a few inches in diameter. Ashes and burned twigs were inside the circle. The Swagman's small, well-shielded campfire.

I saw nothing that resembled clues to murder. I saw nothing that resembled anything except a life of simple abject poverty.

Sherlock Holmes might have solved three crimes on the spot, all while chiding John Watson for not paying closer attention. Poirot would have shuddered at the disorder and dirt but also noticed clues completely invisible to online detectives.

And Spenser would have just come back again or watched and waited until he finally saw something amiss.

The Swagman, I figured, would keep panhandling until the end of rush hour. Then he would come back to camp for a while and do whatever else street-corner beggars did until the start of afternoon rush hour at four o'clock.

I angled away from his camp about fifty yards and found a small clearing behind a thick clump of bushes. I could hide there, I figured, and push some leaves apart, just like a cartoon detective, while I spied on him.

I picked up a long stick and poked and prodded the grass and leaves behind the bushes. Once I was satisfied no snakes or geckos were lurking about, I sat down and waited.

And waited.

My detective training course had offered no information on stakeouts in woods and forests. Once you hunker down to wait, seconds move like minutes.

Your legs quickly go numb. And your brain fills with random, useless thoughts. *Memo to brain*, I forced myself to think. *Remember these points when I write* The Erwin Tennyson Introductory Guide to Foolproof Detection.

A good private eye often did his stakeouts in his car, stoically sitting and watching until his bladder was ready to burst.

Suddenly, I felt that call of nature. My diuretics were kicking in. But I realized I was not facing a big crisis. If a bear could shit in the woods, a detective could pee behind a tree.

I struggled to my feet, shook the numbness out of my legs and stepped over to a nearby scrub oak. I positioned myself behind it and focused on not splashing on my shoes. But just as I got relief started, I glanced up and realized the Swagman now was hurrying back to his camp.

I stopped what I was doing and became a cartoon detective hiding behind a tree.

The Swagman pulled off his backpack, set it down and opened it. He looked around quickly, and I didn't sense that he saw me. He sat down beside his backpack and pulled out something brown and small, with a short strap.

Working quickly and smoothly, he pulled up his right pant leg and fastened the brown object to his ankle. As he worked, I caught a glimpse of a pearl-colored handle.

The Swagman now had an ankle holster and what appeared to be a very compact .25-caliber pistol.

He stood up, looked around again and lifted the back of his shirt. I saw right away that he had another holster in the small of his back. It had what looked like a Glock 23, .40-caliber. It was the right size for the murder weapon.

I knew the homeless often carried knives, clubs and even guns for protection. But the Swagman was packing serious firepower, and he looked mean enough to kill anyone who crossed him.

I figured I was dead if he saw me.

He did not. He adjusted the back holster's position, dropped his shirt, and put on his backpack again. Then he strode out of his camp and headed toward the parking lot again.

Once I saw him cross Lamar Street and walk up a sidewalk that passed alongside a tennis court, I finished my call of nature quickly. Then I broke cover and headed toward my car. I moved quickly through the high grass and leaves, remembering to follow an indirect path.

I wasn't worried anymore about snakes or geckos.

I figured I had just dodged a potential bullet.

FORTY-EIGHT

Back at my apartment, I put on the night locks, closed the drapes and called Sgt. Marklin. He didn't answer his cell phone. I left him a voice message and followed up with a text message. "Please meet me Starbucks ASAP. Urgent."

Then I sat at my kitchen table and sent Joan a text message: "Love u!"

Right away, she sent me a reply: "Luv u 2! C u at 5!"

I remembered she had two house showings this afternoon, both of them with the same investor who kept trying to pick up West Austin properties on the cheap. "I know I won't make a sale," she had said that morning. "But I'll still have to show them. He'll offer twenty-five percent below the asking price, and the owners won't budge."

I flipped back and forth through my detective training manual, but my thoughts stayed focused on the Swagman and his guns. He had the perfect disguise. The cops at the murder scene had ruled him out right away. They seemed to know him, and they ignored his panhandling. There would be no more suspicion of him unless he fled.

After two hours, I finally got a text reply from Sgt. Marklin: "Starbucks in 10."

He was already at my favorite table I arrived. And he had bought me a small iced tea lemonade.

"Two Splendas, right?" he asked as I sat down.

I nodded, trying to look grateful. But I could feel grimness tightening my face.

"So what's urgent," he asked.

Talking very quietly, I told him what I had done and what I had seen, more or less.

Mostly less, actually.

As an unlicensed private…researcher…I had to be very careful with what I said and how I said it, particularly to the police.

Marklin gave me a real-detective's puzzled look.

"Let me get this straight," he said, also keeping his voice level very low. "You were just hiking through the woods this morning and you stopped to pee behind a tree, and you saw this guy – this shaman –"

"Swagman. He's bushy-haired and has a big, black-and-grey beard. He looks a lot like an Australian swagman."

"You saw this swagman, and he's carrying a bunch of guns."

"Just two. One on his ankle, and one in the small of his back."

Sgt. Marklin frowned. "If I didn't know better, Mister Tennyson, I'd think you were maybe following

189

the guy and spying on him. Maybe doing a little *unlicensed* investigating."

I didn't miss his emphasis, nor its implicit threat. He could reach for his handcuffs in about two seconds.

"I didn't tell you all of it," I said, thinking fast. "I'm researching and writing an article on the homeless who camp out in city parks."

There were still distinct advantages to being a newspaper writer, even a laid-off newspaper writer. Sgt. Marklin could never prove that I was *not* researching and writing such an article and hoping to sell it as a freelancer.

Little Paul smirked and relaxed. *The power of the press.*

"Okay, good," he said. "Finish your drink. Let's go out to my car."

"Am I in trouble?" I said.

"Yep. But we can talk more about it outside."

His white cop car had no external markings. But it was packed with radios, clipboards, a shotgun and a computer. He started its engine, turns the air conditioning on full blast and did not turn down the volume on the police radio channels.

He looked at me now and glared. "You're Dad's friend and you're a famous book reviewer."

"Not anymore," I said. "I'm not a famous reviewer. But I *am* your Dad's friend. And yours, too, I hope."

"We're all friends. So I'm gonna say this once and one time only. You came across an undercover cop this morning and damn near compromised an ongoing investigation. That's all I'm gonna say. Keep your ass well out of our way, and keep your fuckin' mouth completely shut about what you saw this morning. Otherwise, I'll have to stick you *under* the fuckin' jail. Do you understand?"

"Yes, sir," I said. "Completely."

"Be sure you do."

The sternness melted from his face. "Dad says you're giving him some good advice for his novel. Keep up the good work."

It was my signal to get out of his car.

"I will," I said.

I stood in the Starbucks parking lot and watched him wheel his Crown Victoria out onto Lamar and head south.

After he was gone, I walked to my car and climbed in and wondered what the hell I could do next.

When I decided, I couldn't believe I would do it. But I figured I had no choice now.

Absolutely no choice.

FORTY-NINE

I drove straight to my private investigator – my private *researcher* – office and called Robert Michaelsohn.

"Is the reviewing position still open?"

Robert was all business. "If you'll help me sell advertising."

My office rent was due again. I owed $19.95 for my subscription to *Private Eye News*, the self-described "*New York Times* of P.I. journals." My laser printer needed a new $59.95 toner cartridge. I still hadn't bought the pint bottle of booze for my top drawer. My next Social Security check was three weeks away. And Joan had emailed me a link to a bracelet she really liked. It was on sale at Nordstrom for just $199.99.

"Yes, I will," I said.

Going over to the dark side was much easier than I had imagined. Especially when the light side's light bulbs were all burned out.

"Good," Robert said. "I just fired the clown who claimed he wrote book reviews for *The Paris Review*."

"What happened?"

"I told him five hundred words max. His first review was four *thousand* five hundred words."

"Damn!"

"I told him to cut it way down. Well, he cut it down to three-thousand-nine-hundred words and said that was his absolute bottom line. A fucking prima donna. I *loved* firing his ass."

"But now you're on deadline again and you need copy that fits."

"That's why I'm hiring you, Erwin. You understand the business."

"And you know I need some money."

"Always a good motivator," Robert said.

One of the best, I had to agree. "What do you need me to do?"

"We're staying focused on Austin authors for now," Robert said. "Do you have any of Frank Arkandale's books?"

"There's only a few that I *don't* have," I said.

"Have you read them?"

"A few of his early ones. None lately."

"Neither have I. Pick out three of his Westerns and three of his science-fiction novels. Give me five hundred words max on each. We'll call it 'Austin's Arkandale: Rounding Up the Best' – some shit like that. Keep the reviews mostly positive, even if you despise the books."

"What's the deadline?"

"Very soon. Have you finished them yet?"

"What?"

Robert laughed. "Seriously, do them as quickly as you can. Send each one as you finish it. I'll post them right away. And be at my office at ten a.m. tomorrow. We'll go out and sell some ads."

"Where's your office?"

"Do you know the Starbucks on Anderson Lane?"

"Yes. Where do I go from there?"

"Right in the front door. I'll have your drink ready," Robert said. "You still drink those sissy tea lemonades?"

FIFTY

I stayed up until 3 a.m., flipping through two of Frank's Westerns and struggling to write something – anything – positive about them.

Southwestern Star was a standard chase-down-the-bad-guy story set deep in the heart of Texas sagebrush country. An ex-U.S. Marshal named Gunn Blandon apparently had quit being an honest lawman and taken up the life of a drunken gambler. But it was all a ruse to get him closer and closer to a sundown shootout with "Bad Irish" Jack O'Toole, the meanest gunslinger west of County Cork *and* the Mississippi River.

In all honesty, I wanted to write: *"Arkandale's characters grunt, snort, growl, spit and gesticulate dialogue that would be bad even in a B-movie.* Southwestern Star *is shallow, predictable escapist fiction that should be read only while traveling on a bus, train or plane – after a week at a plumbers' convention."*

But honest opinion, of course, was not the assignment. Robert needed me to help entice readers to rush to bookstores and blindly buy stacks of books. If that happened, the bookstores' owners would buy more advertising, and Robert and I would split the commissions.

"Frank Arkandale's Southwestern Star *keeps readers riding tall in the saddle in this stirring, satisfying, action-packed Western thriller,"* I wrote.

I also reviewed *Dust Devils* before I fell asleep. But now, as Joan woke me up with a kiss and stuck a warm bran muffin in my mouth, I could not remember anything of what I had said about it, except "*a hard-charging tale with more action than a cattle stampede in the middle of a windblown prairie fire.*"

I sat up in bed, clutched the muffin and chewed. It had raisins and walnuts, my favorites.

Joan already was dressed in her real-estate power lady suit. She stuck a small plate in my other hand. "Don't get any crumbs in the bed," she said.

"What time is it?" I didn't have my glasses on, and the big-digit clock radio on the dresser was an electric blue and plastic-black blur.

"Ten after six," Joan said. "Time to get up and start your new job."

I crawled out from under the covers, carefully balancing the muffin on the plate. If it hit the floor, there would be more muffins in the kitchen. But I would have to vacuum Joan's bedroom after breakfast.

"I don't want to sell advertising. It's commission sales," I said.

Joan smirked at me. "And selling houses is…?" She made little answer-the-question gestures.

"Commission sales. But at least the commission is big."

"It's six percent," Joan said. "Your commission will be fifteen percent."

"But I'll have to sell a bunch of ads. You'll just have to sell one house."

Joan was not sympathetic. "It's all the same process. So, get off your sweet buns and start selling."

She gave me one more kiss and left.

I heard her Infiniti start up and pull out of her driveway as I set the muffin plate on top of the dresser, pulled open a drawer and searched for socks.

That was when I realized: *Dammit, advertising sellers have to wear suits.*

I hated wearing a suit while working.

But Joan already had made sure I had two good ones available: one at my place and one at hers.

I walked over to the closet, opened it and found a freshly ironed white dress shirt and tasteful tie hanging right next to my grey Brooks Brothers two-button business suit.

Joan had put together the ensemble while I slept.

How did I function without her? I wondered.

FIFTY-ONE

Mid-America newspaper staffers have never been known to set, nor follow, sartorial trends.

Robert Michaelsohn looked like a salesman of very used cars as he hunched over his morning coffee. He was wearing tan slacks, brown penny loafers, tan socks and a fuzzy wool sports coat with tiny grey-and-black checks that seemed to shimmer as he moved.

He saw me enter. He slid my iced tea lemonade across the table and gestured at my waiting chair.

"Damn. You look like a bond trader," he said. "Hello, Erwin." He shook my hand.

"Or maybe a mortician." I sat down and wrapped my hand around the cold, sweaty plastic cup. "Joan shamed me into getting rid of my favorite jacket."

"That green thing with the brown elbow patches?"

"I felt very literary when I wore it."

"It made you look like a golf writer. We used to joke about it behind your back."

He made little quote marks in the air. "'*Erwin Tennyson hits another bogey into the mysterious rough with his latest review.*'"

"I gave it to Goodwill."

"Good," Robert said. "Now some homeless guy is walking around looking like a golf writer."

A modified memory flashed into my head. The Swagman emerged from the woods just beyond the running trail, close to where I had found the young woman. This time, he was wearing my old green coat, and it was two sizes too small for him.

"The guys on the sports desk always looked homeless," I said.

Robert sipped his coffee and nodded. "Some of them were. Divorced *and* homeless. Remember Wild Bill Adkins?"

"Barely."

"He covered horse racing and rugby, and he helped out with Friday night high school football. He actually lived at the paper for a couple of months. His wife found out he was having an affair with a sixteen-year-old corn-fed high school cheerleader. She could have had him jailed, but she just threw all of his stuff out into the front yard, set fire to it, and divorced him."

There but for the grace of God – and Joan – go I.

"Ah, the good old days," I said.

"Okay, we can't eat nostalgia. Let's get to work," Robert said. He handed me a list of fifty two potential advertisers for our book review web page. "Today, we'll hit our top five prospects first."

"Book Blast?" I said. "I've never heard of them."

"Not many people have. That's why I'm sure they'll buy an ad from us."

Robert took another drink of coffee and gave me a businesslike look. "I'll tell them first about our six-hundred-dollar half-page special. It's really the best deal."

"What will I do?"

"For now, just nod approvingly and say something like this: *'I would have shopped here sooner if I had known you were here.'* I'll give you a rate sheet tomorrow and send you out on your own."

"And we split thirty percent?"

"On every ad we sell. That's right," Robert said. "If Book Blast buys – and I'm very sure they will – we'll get ninety bucks each just as soon as their check clears."

We finished our drinks, and Robert drove us down MoPac to Cesar Chavez Boulevard. We took the Congress Avenue bridge over Town Lake and found a parking space in an area of trendy bars, Mexican restaurants and small art galleries.

We walked past a donut shop and inhaled its fresh, sugary aromas. "It's right around the corner," Robert said.

"GOING OUT OF BUSINESS – All Books 60% Off."

That was the big sign hanging across Book Blast's front window.

The front door was locked. I peered through the glass. The shelves were empty.

"What's next on the list?" I asked Robert.

We headed back up MoPac, this time to LiteraryLand. It was a new-and-used bookstore in a strip shopping mall in suburban Round Rock.

"It's been in business for twenty-two years," Robert said. "They do a lot of advertising."

We pulled into a parking space right in front of the correct address.

LiteraryLand now was an empty storefront with a "For Lease" sign.

I looked at Robert. He looked at his list and kept looking at it.

"Shit," he said quietly.

We had better luck at our fifth stop, Jack's Paperbacks, an old two-bedroom house on East 12th Street crammed with worn romance novels, Westerns, science-fiction books and detective potboilers.

Robert sent me inside alone while he remained in his car and used his cell phone to try to set up some sales appointments.

Jack Adair, in his seventies and crippled with arthritis and gout, listened quietly to my fumbling sale pitch. Then he nodded and bought a ten-dollar "Inventory Reduction Sale" classified ad. "All books 90% off!"

"I ought to burn this goddam place down," Jack said to me as he wrote out the check with an unsteady hand. "It would make one hell of a fire. Might even make the *Statesma*n's front page. Nobody's buying shit anymore. Goddam Bush recession. I could just sit right in here while it all burned and give myself a Viking funeral. Solve a lot of problems at one time."

"Thank you," I said as he handed me the check. I didn't know what else to say. But, impulsively, I picked up two worn books from the top of a small pile on his counter – a Western and a teen romance. "I'll buy these."

Jack took them from me and flipped them over. While he squinted at the tiny cover prices, I pulled two bucks out of my wallet. At ninety-percent off, I figured they would cost me less than a buck-fifty and perhaps encourage Jack to buy a bigger ad from me next time.

"That'll be eight bucks," Jack said.

"Eight?" I couldn't hide the surprise in my voice.

"The sale doesn't start until you run the ad," Jack said.

FIFTY-TWO

Robert was leaving someone a voice message as I climbed into his car.

"We'll be in your area until four o'clock, so give us a call," he said.

He punched the end-call button and blew out his breath as he looked at me. "How'd you do in there?"

"Jack bought a ten-dollar classified."

"Well, that's something, I guess. What are those?" He took the two paperbacks from my hand and looked at them. "*Dust Riders* and *Mollie Gets a Boyfriend.* Did he give you these?"

I confessed what I had done and why.

Robert scowled. "So we made a buck-sixty apiece on the ad, but you spent eight bucks on two books you'll never read, and I've burned up a lot of four-dollar gasoline just getting us here."

"What's our next stop?" I said.

Robert stared out the windshield for a long moment. His eyes seemed to be focused somewhere beyond the aging neighborhood outside.

"We don't have one," he said finally.

"You have a list."

"I've made a lot of calls, but so far, nobody wants us to stop by."

"So what do we do next?"

"I've just made an executive-level decision," Robert said, finally. "This isn't going to work out for either of us. I'm sorry."

"What do you mean?"

"I mean, I'm sorry, Erwin. I'm going to have to let you go."

"But I just sold an ad. We can *do* this. The next stop may be the big one."

"I assured the investor I could bring in at least a thousand a week on ad sales. Enough to pay me, pay you and pay him a nice little return on his money."

"We haven't even finished trying the first list."

Robert tore the list into small pieces and tossed them out his window.

"We have now," he said. "You're fired, and I quit. Get out of my car."

"My car's back at Starbucks. Can't you give a ride?"

Robert looked out the driver's-side window.

"There's a bus stop across the street. I gotta get out of town and think."

"You're joking," I said.

"No, I'm not," he said. "Get out *now*."

I climbed out of Robert's car and carefully closed his door.

He slammed his car into gear and raced away, squealing his tires, heading south. He appeared, indeed, to be heading out of town.

I looked down the block and saw a bus coming. I tossed the two paperbacks into an open recycling bin on Jack's sidewalk and imagined his building engulfed in flames as I walked across the street.

A hundred thousand unwanted paperbacks indeed would make one hell of a Viking fire.

Maybe I could sit inside with Jack and take notes until the last minute, until the flames and smoke threatened my survival.

Then I could rush outside, reporter's notebook in hand, and – do what?

Blog about it?

Tweet?

FIFTY-THREE

I got off the #1 Cap Metro bus at the corner of 45th and Guadalupe and walked a half mile west to the Starbucks at 44th and Lamar.

I had tried very hard to hate Robert Michaelson while I rode next to a college student who kept humming and gyrating to his iPod and directly across the bus aisle from a painfully thin old man who kept muttering to himself. He was incoherent except when he suddenly said, very clearly: "Cotton burgers."

Had he meant "cotton burghers"? Sherlock Holmes would have found this strange notion worthy of deeper investigation. He would have stayed on the bus, followed the old man home, hid and waited somewhere near his shabby apartment, and eventually solved a murder that no doubt had long stumped the Austin Police Department *and* Scotland Yard.

But I was not Holmes. I was just glad to return to my loyal Sunfire in the Starbucks parking lot.

It wasn't there. There was only one other dirty blue, somewhat sporty sedan. A Ford Mustang.

I walked quickly through the parking lot, looking at the rows of cars, even trying mentally to change some of their colors from grey or red or white to blue.

Just as I panicked and contemplated calling the police, that's when I remembered.

Robert and I had left from another Starbucks, the one on West Anderson Lane. It was a four-mile walk from this one.

I called Joan's cell phone and got her "I'm in a meeting with a client" voice mail message. I hung up without saying anything and checked my pockets and wallet for cash. I didn't have enough to pay a cabbie. I didn't even have enough for another bus ride. I dreaded walking a solid hour north on 63-year-old legs.

Just as I took the first step to hike, however, I heard my name called behind me.

"Erwin!"

I looked around. Big Paul was leaving the coffee shop with his computer bag in one hand and a to-go coffee in the other.

"Lose something? I've been watching you march around."

Feeling sheepish and keeping the details to a minimum as he walked up, I explained what had happened.

"Hell, I do shit like that all the time," he said. "I'm surprised Little Paul hasn't had me committed already. Yesterday, I left my phone at home, and then I locked myself out of my car. I tried to call Little Paul from a phone booth, but I didn't have any change. Come on, I'll give you a ride."

"Is it safe?" I said, feeling relieved and trying to make a joke.

"Oh, hell, no," he said. "Most of my whole career, I was the Ranger in the passenger seat. My partners always drove."

Ten minutes later, when he dropped me off right behind my car, I thanked him, climbed out and immediately made a mental note.

Never ride with him again.

Big Paul apparently had forgotten he was no longer the Ranger *not* behind the steering wheel. While he regaled me with a Ranger story about chasing loose cattle and described a scene from his unfinished novel, he ran through two stop signs and a red light, nearly hit two bicyclists and slowed down to just 40 as we went through an active, 20-mph school zone.

No matter how many times I stomped on the imaginary brake on the passenger side, it made absolutely no difference to his driving or his attention span.

Never ride with him again!

FIFTY-FOUR

Early the next morning, while Joan slept, I pulled on my favorite faded blue jeans and plain brown T-shirt and slipped my feet into my favorite "Made in China" compressed-foam flip-flops.

I decided to surprise her by serving breakfast in bed. I went into my kitchen, found my one serving tray and loaded it up with one of my two cloth napkins, a day-old croissant from Upper Crust Bakery, one egg a la Erwin (hard-scrambled) and a cup of coffee that immediately made her wince.

"Strong, huh?" I said.

Joan sat up straighter in bed and took another tentative sip. She winced again and carefully set the coffee cup back on the tray on her bed stand.

"I love you dearly, and I'm grateful for this sweet breakfast," she said. "But honestly, Erwin Tennyson, you make *the* worst coffee on Planet Earth."

"Well, would you like a cup of tea?" I said.

She smiled and nodded as she tasted her egg and croissant. "These are fine. Thank you."

As I headed toward the kitchen, she called me back. "I have a better idea. Why not be a dear, drive over to Starbucks and get me a coffee while I take a shower? I'll buy you an iced tea, if you will."

She opened her purse and pulled out her Starbucks gold card.

Burnet Road and Lamar Boulevard were both crowded with cars, buses, motorcyclists and bicyclists, all trying impatiently to get to work. As I steered, dodged and braked, I felt happy and lucky that I no longer had to participate in the 8 a.m. and 5 p.m. parades.

When I returned, she was dressed in a new, dark-blue, three-button businesswoman's suit, with sensible dark-blue heels and a white silk blouse. It all went very well with her recently enhanced blonde hair.

"You look like the proverbial million bucks," I said, handing over her coffee. I meant it.

She smiled demurely, sniffed the coffee's aroma and nodded her satisfaction.

"Thanks, but the house I'm showing today is priced at two million five."

I pulled her toward me very carefully and gave her a non-coffee-spilling kiss. "Then I stand corrected. You look like the proverbial *three* million bucks." I meant that, too.

"I love it when you lie--" Joan said as she gave me a playful return kiss.

"I'm not lying."

"—in bed. And I lie in bed. And we both lie in bed. And sometimes we do more than just lie there."

"A *lot* more," I said. "Especially for an old guy who now qualifies for the senior-citizen discounts at movie theaters, barber shops and restaurants."

"Oh, poo, you're not old," Joan said.

"That's exactly what I told Harry S Truman the day I was born."

Joan kissed me again. "My place tonight. Win, lose or draw, I'm serving pasta, marinara sauce, salad, fresh Italian bread, an unpretentious little red wine, some nice French cheese *and* a few pieces of Belgian chocolate."

"Wow. What can I bring?" I said.

Joan picked up her real estate briefcase.

"Just bring the one thing you never forget," Joan said.

She chuckled and winked at me as she went out my front door.

FIFTY-FIVE

I lingered at home and read every page of the *Austin Daily Democrat* and the *Austin America-Statesman*. The news was pretty much the same in both newspapers: riots overseas; continuing economic crisis at home; and the ultraconservative Texas Legislature dealing with the massive state budget deficit by trying to tighten abortion restrictions, give early releases to terminally ill prisoners so they could die at their own expense, and other reduce or eliminate services and assistance to the poor.

Later in the morning, I went to my office and soon found myself embroiled in a missing-dog case. Actually, it wasn't a case that required any investigative skills. The dog, in fact, did most of the work.

I had been sitting at my desk for about thirty minutes, trying again to doodle up solutions to the mystery behind Marisol Alfaro's death. Suddenly, I heard a scratching noise and a whining whimper right outside my front door.

I opened the door, and a very small dog – a white, black and brown rat terrier – raced inside, ran straight to a back corner of the room, turned around in frantic circle several times and plopped down onto the floor. Almost immediately, it went to sleep, seemingly very much at home.

Was this an omen of good fortune or merely one more distracting complication? The dog had no collar. Had it been dumped, abandoned? Had it run away from an abusive home?

I didn't want the responsibility of a pet. Yet, after decades of writing mystery novel reviews for newspapers, I couldn't forget how a series of German short-haired pointers named Pearl figure prominently into the lifestyle and sometimes the investigations of Robert B. Parker's best-selling pugilistic detective, Spenser.

And in Dean Koontz's 1997 mystery thriller, *Fear Nothing*, the hero, Christopher Snow, needed his black Labrador retriever, Orson, to help him unravel a complex military conspiracy.

Even Sherlock Holmes sometimes relied on a dog to help him solve a crime. In *The Sign of the Four*, for example, Sir Arthur Conan Doyle's second novel, Holmes sticks a creosote-stained handkerchief under the nose of a fluffy-legged canine and declares: "Here you are, doggy! Good old Toby! Smell it, Toby, smell it!" Then Holmes and Watson chase after the mutt as it tries to follow the bad guys' trail.

Maybe I could keep the dog on a leash and call him – her? – "Toby." Terriers were an intelligent breed. Perhaps it could lead me straight to clues and evidence.

I called Joan for a quick second opinion.

"No," she said. "Not only no but hell no."

"Why?" I said.

"I like the idea, the *concept*, of pets, Erwin. But not the responsibility, the veterinary bills, and the backyard funerals. Anyway, I'm allergic to dog hair and cat dander."

"What if I keep Toby at my office, as a kind of watchdog?"

"I hope you enjoy cleaning up dog poop and dog pee every morning and taking the dog out for frequent walks. And what's the pet deposit in that complex?"

I opened my filing cabinet and pulled out the lease agreement I had barely read before signing. Pets, it said, were "discouraged." But if a business owner insisted on keeping some kind of animal in his or her office, a pet deposit of $1,000 was required and was only partially refundable after all "damages and stains" were deducted.

"Okay, no dog," I said.

I promised Joan I would help the terrier find a good home.

"Good," she said. "I'd hate having to compete with a dog for your time and attention."

We ended our call, and I let the dog sleep while I contemplated how to get rid of it.

I could take it to a veterinarian to be scanned for a micro-chip and maybe discover its owner. I could buy a "Found Dog" classified ad. I could email some of my contacts; maybe Big Paul needed a little dog to help keep him company. I could just push it out the door first and hope that it somehow found its way home. Or I could call animal control to come get it and take it away – to doggie death row?

No, that last one I would not do.

While I was contemplating these choices, a folded flyer suddenly was thrust through the mail slot in my front door.

"Reward!" it said. "Missing Dog! No questions asked!" The flyer had been photocopied, but there was no mistaking the photo. It was Toby.

Except Toby's real name, apparently, was "Princess Missy."

I called the flyer's phone number. Princess Missy's owner was just a few doors down, still thrusting flyers through mail slots.

Less than a minute later, a stout woman in her forties opened my office door.

"There you are!" she said, looking past me. The dog woke up, stared at her and quickly got into a defensive crouch. It tried to back up, but it was stopped by the wall.

The woman strode inside, scooped up the rat terrier and held it tight. It trembled in her grasp and did not look exactly glad to see her.

"He – she – came to my door and wanted in," I said, "so I let it in. I was trying to figure out how to find the owner when I got your flyer."

The woman gave me a sharp, sour look. "That's a lie! Princess Missy would *never* go inside a strange office," she said. "I think you grabbed her, and you were planning to keep her. Or sell her to one of those terrible labs that does medical experiments on dogs."

"That's ridiculous," I said. "Toby – Princess What's-Her-Name – wanted in, so I let him – her – in."

"Toby? You gave my dog another *name*? That's proof you kidnapped her! I'm going to call the police!"

She started digging in her purse for what I hoped was her cell phone, not a stylish little pearl-handled .25.

I still had the squirt gun Joan had given me. But its ammunition now was completely dried up. Could I grab it and throw it in time to make a strong-arm play for the pistol?

She pulled out a cell phone that was even older and less stylish than mine.

"Madam!" I said sternly. I tried to channel what I hoped was Sam Spade's meanest voice – or at least Dashiell Hammett's. "I am a private de – *researcher*. I have friends on the police force. And I know some Texas Rangers. They will all testify that I did not steal your dog."

Of course, Little Paul might actually say that I did, just so he could put me under the jail for a night.

"Come on, Princess Missy, let's go," the woman said to her little dog. She held it protectively to her chest with two hands, the same way a fullback clutches a football as he starts a two-yard plunge. "Let's get away from this bad man."

Toby – Princess Missy – barked and growled at me right on cue as they moved past me

I snatched up her flyer and held it out like a restraining order. "You said 'Reward.' I found your dog. Where's my reward?"

The woman now clutched her terrier with one hand, like a wide receiver moving the ball through open field. With her other hand, she yanked open my office door.

"Your reward is, I won't call the police!"

And your reward... I wanted to say. My brain tried to conjure up the rudest words it could organize. But common sense, plus my training from the Advanced Online School of Private Investigation, suddenly and firmly kicked in.

Say absolutely nothing that could be construed as a "terroristic threat" under Section 22.07 of the Texas Penal Code.

"Have a *whatever* day!" I said. I slammed my office door closed behind her – and locked it firmly from inside.

The Case of the Missing Dog Formerly and Briefly Known as Toby was solved. But it did not merit a folder labeled "Case 003." Nor had it brought me any income, repeat business or referrals.

I wadded up the missing-dog flyer and arced a right-handed hook shot toward the office trash can. The paper ball hit the sweet spot of the "backboard" and tumbled right into the can.

Two points! Tennyson scores!

Someone suddenly knocked loudly on my office door. I looked through the peephole, fully expecting to see a cop. Or Princess Missy's queen mother again. Maybe both.

It was Karen. I opened the door and gestured for her to come in. "Welcome!"

She stayed put. "Don't forget your office rent is due in the office by five o'clock today, Mister Tennyson." She gave me a quick, business-like smile and made a check mark on her clipboard. Then she walked off, her heels clicking on the sidewalk as she headed toward the next occupied office.

FIFTY-SIX

The next day, I stayed at Joan's house after she went to work. I sat at her big dining room table and scribbled notes on a yellow legal pad.

I wrote "NOVEL" at the top of the first page and drew a box around it.

Then, three lines down, I wrote a tentative title, "Second Notice," and drew a box around it, too.

P.D. James had opened her complex mystery novel *A Certain Justice* with the words: "Murderers do not usually give their victims notice." Of course, the detective in this case is Commander Adam Dalgliesh of Scotland Yard, he of strong logic and a troubled staff ready to help and hinder him.

Perhaps I could go against that grain. The victim in my novel could get not just one notice but two. Maybe three. And the police detective could be a lone wolf out of necessity, because of staff cutbacks. He could be something like Philip Marlowe but prone to outbursts of illogic.

I started outlining a novel that I figured would please Frank – perhaps his publisher, too.

It was good to have a friend in high places.

Chapter 1: Introduce detective. Call him what – Ishmael? Clark Kant? Sam Shovel? Get serious! Thomas J. Banquo, resisting evil wherever he sees it?

We meet T.J. Banquo investigating Case A: A young woman is dead in a park. Looks like suicide. Banquo suspects it's not. Wants to dig deeper. But his cell phone rings. New case, ASAP, supervisor says. A police informant working undercover as a drug mule has been found dead, stabbed repeatedly inside a South Austin house, clutching a blood-stained note: "This is your second notice." Mexican cartel? Local gang? Dissatisfied customer? Desperate junkie? Murderous slumlord trying to collect past-due rent?

So far, so good, I thought. A detective, victim *and* a mystery. I made myself a peanut butter-and-strawberry preserves sandwich, poured a glass of chocolate soy milk and moved on to the next chapter.

Chapter 2: Something odd and unexpected happens.

That was all I had after I finished the sandwich and soy milk. I decided to push ahead and come back to Chapter 2 later.

Chapter 3: Banquo meets a beautiful woman, a French Interpol detective working undercover in Austin. He and she spend an intense night working under his covers before they start comparing notes on their current cases. They find that they have some kind of nexus or intersection or commonality: They're both looking for the same killer. They team up and create a dangerous pairing of skills and sex. Her name is Yvette Something – research French names.

Joan had left three chocolate-covered strawberries in a covered dish. I ate one, the extra one that she would insist I have.

Chapter 4: They go to Paris, where…something happens. What?

Chapter 5: In the 15th, just a block from a Metro stop, something really, really bad happens, but what??? To whom? Why? What do T.J. and Yvette do about it?

I stared at the notepad and tried to be honest with myself. I knew a few basic things about how an Austin, Texas, police detective worked and talked. I knew nothing about Interpol or French women or French detectives or drugs. I could research all of this. I was, after all, Erwin Tennyson, private researcher. But I didn't want to. I wanted to find the real killer of the real Marisol Alfaro.

I ripped the sheet from the notepad, tore it into shreds and made myself another PB&J with strawberry preserves.

It was a strawberry kind of day. That was all I really knew for sure.

FIFTY-SEVEN

I told Joan nothing about the novel, before or after we made love. I knew she would side with Frank, whom she had not yet met, and she would expect me to write it.

The next morning, she left my apartment just after dawn. A desperate rancher had called her yesterday wanting to sell a thousand acres. His ranch was a hundred miles west of Austin, in the middle of what he called "God's country." On the map, it was known only to God and could be found only with a GPS and detailed instructions via email: "…then take the rutted path between the two dead trees and drive three miles south to the house. I'll be there with my wife, my dogs and my attorney."

Normally, Joan tried to stay away from handling land deals. But with the single-family home market still in the recessionary doldrums and banks not making loans, she was looking at all possibilities and sometimes taking deals she normally avoided. Yesterday, she had helped a college student locate a new apartment and collected a hundred-dollar commission from the complex's manager.

"Gas money for a week," she had told me as we ate the frozen dinners I had lovingly microwaved.

Soon after she left, I went outside in my underwear and flip-flops and quickly retrieved the *Austin*

American-Statesman. The front-page headline startled me awake.

Undercover Cops Smash
Panhandler Crime Ring

The article detailed how a six-month undercover investigation had just led to the arrest of sixteen men and women who had posed as homeless beggars. They had stood at intersections with tales of woe written on cardboard signs. In reality, they sold illegal drugs to certain drive-by customers, while also collecting tax-free cash from Austin's large army of unsuspecting good Samaritans.

"These are heartless scum who do more than just traffic in illegal substances," Austin Police Chief Benjamin Zann said in the article. "They also take criminal advantage of our most helpless and unfortunate citizens, the homeless and unemployed, for whom every day is a fight for survival."

The chief praised "the brave efforts of a courageous team of investigators led by one of our top detective sergeants."

Later that morning, as I sat at my favorite table, sucking down my morning iced tea lemonade, Little Paul came into Starbucks for a cup of caffeine to go.

He nodded at me and stopped at my table as he poured three sugar packets into his coffee.

"Congratulations," I said quietly.

"Thank you," he said. He pulled out a chair and sat down. "I've canceled your reservation."

"My reservation for what?" I said, puzzled.

"For the cell under the jail. Remember? We have one, you know."

Little Paul took a sip of his coffee and grinned.

"We call it the Hell Cell. It makes solitary confinement seem like a Miami Beach vacation."

"You're kidding," I said.

"Maybe I am, maybe I'm not," Little Paul said. "You won't get to find out, *this* time."

I didn't tell him anything at all about the lost and found dog.

He took another sip of his coffee and stared out the windows for a moment at the traffic passing on Lamar Boulevard. Then he looked right at me. "Got any leads on the woman in the park?"

I stared back, trying to read his expression and his eyes. I also glanced at his free hand. His handcuffs were on that side of his gun belt. "I'm not investigating," I said, intending to say more.

He cut me off. "You research things, I know that. Has your *research* turned up anything that might help us?"

As I studied his face, the stern set of his mouth and the intensity of his waiting stare, I considered my answer very carefully. I had, thus far, turned up absolutely nothing that had helped anyone with anything.

No, belay that, I thought, mentally lapsing into long-ago Navy speak. Indirectly, at least, I had helped get a failed P.I. named Lazarus Popkin tossed into the Gulf of Mexico. With Joan's grudging help, I had discovered that Karen's mother was about to buy a suburban lot that was several square feet bigger than its plat indicated. Then I had found that stupid dog. Or it had found me and almost gotten me arrested.

The great fictional detective Ellery Queen, facing me across the table in this situation, might have intoned: "Well, I think I know what happened. Do you? Who do you think killed Marisol Alfaro? Did she have a split personality and one part of her murdered the other parts of herself? Did Rich Garpmann get away with murder simply by moving to Oregon? How about the undercover cop who disguised himself as the Swagman? Did he kill her in a fit of self-defense because she was about to compromise his cover? I'll tell you one thing, Erwin: the killer made a mistake. Do you know what it is? I think I do. But I'll wait and see if you figure out what it is."

Actually, I was facing the same dilemma Dashiell Hammett's Sam Spade faced in *The Thin Man*: "The problem with putting two and two together is that sometimes you get four, and sometimes you get twenty-two."

I was trying to put together everything I had, and it all added up to zero, no matter how I arranged it.

It was Colonel Mustard, In the library. With the flash drive.

That's what I wanted to tell Little Paul

But I still had not told him or Big Paul about the drive and its file.

Spenser in this predicament would have Captain Quirk threatening to take away his private investigator's license if he didn't say something quick. I had nothing at all to take away. But the hell cell was still under the jail. And Sgt. Marklin had his ever-ready silver handcuffs on his belt.

Maybe it was time now to get my real estate broker's license and try being Mister Homes instead of Mister Holmes.

"I've got zip," I lied.

FIFTY-EIGHT

"Where *is* your head?" Joan said. "Pay attention!"

I looked at her and then at where she was staring.

I had just poured chocolate sauce instead of barbecue sauce onto the pork chops that I was supposed to put into my oven.

I stared at the dinner chops, feeling helpless and stupid.

Joan grabbed them, thrust them under cold, running water and then patted them dry with paper towels. Working quickly, she re-seasoned the meat, pulled the barbecue sauce from the refrigerator and applied it, and rearranged the chops on the broiler pan.

"Open door, insert chops," she said. "And after that, please go back to your computer and think about that murder case."

"Are you sure?" I said. I put the pork chops in the oven.

As I straightened up, Joan wrapped her arms around me and pulled me into a long kiss. "Sorry," she said. "Sometimes I get jealous of the things that distract you."

"You distract me," I said, "in many wonderful ways."

She smiled but quickly looked serious again. "I haven't wanted you to be a private detective."

"I've noticed," I said, smiling.

She put two fingers to my lips. "Just listen. I've wanted you to just sit in your room and write poetry and novels. I don't want you to get hurt, and I don't want you to get into any kind of trouble."

I tried to say something, but she put the two fingers to my lips again.

"I'm not finished," she said. "I've been trying to keep you under glass, like a butterfly or a ship in a bottle. That's not fair. You have to be who you are, who you want to be. You've never tried to stop me from doing anything."

I gave her a kiss of forgiveness and let my hands slowly slide down from her waist.

"So you'll be my sidekick – my Doctor Watson?"

My hands followed the smooth curvature of her caboose and ended up gently pressing at the top rear of her thighs.

"Absolutely…not," she said, grinning.

She reached back, grabbed my hands and pulled them back up to her waist. "But if you'll ask me very, very nicely, I *might* be willing to consider being your dessert."

Later that evening, while Joan slept peacefully in my bedroom, I sat at my computer and tried to think of good reasons to let the dead woman go.

I was not *really* a detective, just someone who had taken a course and printed out a certificate.

And I was not really *investigating* her death. Just *researching* it. Yet risking arrest for being an unlicensed private eye.

I had turned up exactly two suspects, and they were not suspects at all.

I had almost compromised an Austin Police undercover investigation. Fortunately, that investigation now was over. The *American-Statesman* and *Daily Democrat* both had run front-page stories this morning about the successful roundup of an organized crime ring that had used fake panhandlers to gather donations at intersections. The ring also had robbed real panhandlers and stolen charitable donation collection boxes from stores and churches.

I had found a lost or discarded flash drive with somebody's novel on it, written in Esperanto, which guaranteed little or no readership.

I had found some Esperanto translation software and converted the novel to English. Then I had tried to read it, seeking clues, and I had quickly quit in disgust. It hadn't taken me long to detect that I cared nothing – less than nothing, actually – about swords-and-sandals sagas, especially those set in outer space.

I couldn't imagine Frank Arkandale caring about such novels, either. Yet, that's what his latest best-seller was – and precisely why I had *not* read it.

How can he write that horseshit and face himself in the mirror…all the way to the bank?

I moved over to the refrigerator, poured myself a midnight glass of ginger ale and felt its sparkly bubbles tickle my nose as I took a swallow.

The universe was infinitely large, yes. So there *could* be swords-and-sandals battles happening at this very moment in space. There could be Old West-style shootouts on planets circling Tau Ceti or Betelgeuse.

There could even be, on some obscure, distant world, another unlicensed private detective named Erwin Tennyson drinking ginger ale precisely at this instant.

But I still thought of Frank just as a writer of traditional, down-to-Earth Westerns. That was how he had first achieved his now-vast fame.

Anyway, how could he keep pulling so many stories out of his head? And what was the point? He now had more money than God, and he recently told me he considered his latest books "just some quick new sops for the fan base."

If he's doing it just for the money, and making it by the boatload, why the hell can't I bring in a few bucks, too?

I walked over to my bookshelves and stared at the rows of hardbacks and paperbacks. I found Frank's *High Noon on Neptune* and flipped it open. I skipped the first few pages and scanned the middle of Chapter 1.

Efficient reviewer that I am, I opened a WordPad screen and typed in a few rough notes.

"Somebody named Karchpo, exiled leader of the Twentieth Moon of Narknanya, is in love with Narknanya's queen, who is being held hostage on the Seventeenth Moon. And she will not be released unless the Six-Dimensional Sword of Urrgamah is given over to somebody named Barmog. Otherwise, Barmog will marry the queen against her wishes and...blah, blah, blah."

It sounded exactly like something I had read somewhere before in some other book.

That's when it occurred to me: *This crap is all just alike!*

I saved and closed the file. Then I closed Frank's book, tossed it to the floor and went into the bedroom. I took off my clothes and crawled into bed next to Joan.

She woke just long enough to snuggle against me and ask why I was still awake.

"I'm learning how to write space fantasy novels," I said.

"That's nice," Joan said, not really awake. "You're my fantasy."

She turned on her side and was asleep again in seconds.

I slipped one hand over her side and felt her warm softness and shallow breathing.

Gently, I pulled her closer to me and pressed my face against her hair.

"You're my fantasy, too," I said, too quietly to wake her.

FIFTY-NINE

I did not sleep well. I kept having waking dreams.

And the harder I tried to shut off my mind, the more I thought about Marisol Alfaro and the absurdity of swords and sandals in space.

Weird scenarios kept evolving and dissolving in my head. In one of them, Joan and I were on some barren planet, wearing nothing but sandals and wielding big swords. Hers was bigger than mine, but mine was the jewel-encrusted Six Dimensional Sword of Oogamooga, which everyone in eight universes seemed to covet. It could slice through moon rocks and green cheese just by thinking about it.

I had just cut my finger on it, and now I was looking around for a bandage. "If we had worn our togas, you could have torn off a piece and made a tourniquet," I said to Joan.

"Shut up and fight," she said, ignoring my complaint and staring past me.

I turned and looked at what she was seeing. Frank and Marisol were advancing toward us, dressed like Roman centurions.

"Hey, Frank, how's it going?" I said.

Frank and Marisol raised their swords.

"Kill them," Frank said with a robot-like voice. "Seize the Six-Dimensional Sword of Oogamooga."

Marisol moved toward us like a robot with three dark eyes. "Kill…kill…kill," she said with a flat, emotionless voice.

I raised my terrible, swift sword, the fearsome Oogamooga. But Joan jumped in front of me and brought her sword straight down on top of Marisol's head, splitting her neatly in half and showering the moon soil with robot circuit boards, wiring harnesses and an assortment of servos, gears and springs.

"See, you *can* write this shit," Frank said in his regular voice. He was smiling now and looking at me like a proud father.

I got out of bed and went back to my bookshelves. If I read some Aristotle, Shakespeare or Zola for a few minutes, I figured I could flush the swords and sandals out of my head.

Instead, I grabbed *High Noon on Neptune* again, and this time I vowed to read it word by word, cover to cover. I would divine the secret of Frank's outrageous success, even if it killed me, and figure out how to write a best-seller, too.

"The small bright star rose from behind a mountain."

I read the book's first sentence again and stopped, amazed at what I was seeing. *All of this space fantasy stuff really* is *just alike. Is it all just one story that everyone rewrites?*

I carried the book over to my computer and opened the translated *luna_es.doc* file.

I had written a brief summary of its opening pages as I struggled through them.

"Parchko, exiled leader of the Twelfth Moon of Quarktune, is in love with Quarktune's queen, who is being held hostage on Quarktune's Seventh Moon. And she will not be released unless the Six-Dimensional Sword of Urrgham is given to somebody named Mogbar, who wants to marry the queen against her wishes, etc."

I opened a separate window and pulled up the notes I had made about Frank's novel.

"Somebody named Karchpo is the exiled leader of the Twentieth Moon of Neptune. He is in love with Neptune's queen, who's being held hostage on the Seventeenth Moon. And she will not be freed unless the Six-Dimensional Sword of Urrgamah is given over to somebody named Barmog. Otherwise, Barmog will force the queen to marry him and...blah, blah, blah."

I scrolled deeper into the *luna_es.doc* file.

I looked at the beginnings of three more chapters and compared them with the ways Frank had opened his chapters.

The similarities stunned me. And they led me straight to a strong – Sherlock Holmes would say *invigorating* – conclusion.

Marisol Alfaro had plagiarized Frank's manuscript and translated it into Esperanto to try to hide her crime.

Then, in a fit of deep literary shame, she had shot herself in the head.

And someone passing by had stolen her gun.

Grinning, I crawled into bed again, snuggled against Joan and let her know I had solved the case.

"Mrrrf," she said, not waking up.

I felt, at long last, like a real detective.

SIXTY

"Frank will be *very* impressed when I tell him," I said to Joan the next morning.

We had overslept. Now she was running late to a showing, a $739,000 house in the hills just west of downtown, recently marked down from $819,000. I told her how I finally solved the case, but she barely listened as she yanked on her panty hose and put on her sleek black suit and Jimmy Choos

She quickly checked the papers in her leather briefcase and snapped it closed. "Shouldn't you tell the police, Sergeant What's-His-Name?"

"Marklin. I'll let him know," I said.

Joan grabbed a breakfast cereal bar from my kitchen cabinet, gave me a quick kiss and headed for the door.

"I have two other showings today," she said, standing in the open doorway. "And then I have to go by Atomic Title and help them figure out some closing documents that were faxed with pages missing. And there's probably something else. I'll have to check my book. I may not see you until seven. Bye."

She blew me a quick kiss and closed the door. I listened to her heels click down the stairs to the parking lot. I peeked out the curtain and watched as she backed out in her Infiniti and drove away.

I went to Starbucks, got an iced tea lemonade and waited for Little Paul to come in for his morning coffee. I knew I would have to be very careful how I explained what I had found. I would have to let Sgt. Marklin "solve" the case with my "research."

Little Paul did not show up. I called his cell phone. No answer. I left a voice mail saying that I had some "information" for him.

I called Big Paul. "Sorry, Erwin," he said. "I'm having my prostate tested for the Big C. The nurse is waving me in."

"Where's Little Paul?" I said.

"Houston. Testifying at a trial. He'll be back tomorrow, maybe."

"Thanks. Good luck with the Big C," I said.

"I'll need it," Big Paul said.

I called Frank. His voice mail answered. "I'm in Chicago this morning. I'll be back in Austin late this afternoon."

I left him a message saying I wanted to tell him something important, in person, once he was back in town.

At my detective office, I pulled out the case folder and reviewed its sparse notes.

The more I thought about it, however, the more certain I felt I was completely right. I wondered what Little Paul would say to Marisol Alfaro's family after I told him. Or would he just talk with an El Salvadoran police detective and let him or her break the bad news?

Big Paul, I'm sure, would at least give a grudging nod to my rookie investigative success.

Frank was the big question mark. Would he now quit harping at me to write a novel? Or would he just shrug, open another Shiner and tell me about his latest exploits in New York or Hollywood? What if he turned out to be actually impressed with something I had done?

I straightened up my detective desk. Then I pulled out a fresh file folder, labeled it "Case 003" and put it in my "IN" box. I leaned back in my detective chair and started to daydream about what that next case might be.

My door suddenly opened. Karen entered. Without a word, she handed me a sheet of paper and went out again.

"Notice," the bold headline declared at the top of the page.

I noticed it.

I scanned the letter quickly, picking out key phrases: "...because of rising expenses...ten percent rent increase...effective thirty days from today...pay with cash or money orders only...no longer accepting checks or credit cards for rental payments. Thank you. The Management."

I tried, but could not think of a single detective novel in which the private eye suddenly had to worry about an office rent increase just after he had cracked a big case.

For that matter, had there *ever* been a written moment in which Hammer, Spenser, Spade, Marlowe, Poirot, Queen or any other of the big fictional private eyes deposited their office rent money into a building manager's outstretched hand?

SIXTY-ONE

Frank laughed.

"Esperanto plagiarism? That's your big case?"

He kept chuckling as he opened his second bottle of Shiner beer.

"I'd believe Eskimo plagiarism long before I'd believe anything involving Esperanto," he said.

"I can prove it, Frank, and here's the best part. I'm turning my information and findings over to the Austin Police Department tomorrow morning," I said. "They can take it from there."

Frank started to drink from the second bottle but stopped, set it down carefully and gave me quizzical look.

Something I had just said had somehow gotten past his smug self-centeredness. His face took on an expression I had never seen before. His bushy, grey-and-white eyebrows tightened. "How much have you told them so far?"

"Not much," I said. "I had some suspicions that didn't pan out. But now I'm sure I'm on the right track."

Frank smirked, put down his beer and reached down toward his pants. Suddenly, I realized he was he was pointing something at me. Something beloved by many old-time Marines and sailors.

A Colt .45 semi-automatic, model M1911. *"…recoil-operated, magazine-fed, single-action pistol…seven-round capacity."* I still remembered the ancient litany from Navy boot camp.

"What are you doing?" I said, gesturing at the gun.

It was the same handgun that Mickey Spillane's Mike Hammer carried in a shoulder harness under his left arm. He called his "Betsy."

"Well, Er, believe it or not, you're a better detective than I thought you'd be," Frank said.

I barely heard his praise.

The hole in the gun barrel looked like the business end of a bazooka, or mortar, or 16-inch battleship gun. At this range, it didn't matter which. Anything that came out would blow me into the next universe, with no need of a sword. Or sandals.

"Why?" I said. "Why are you doing this?"

"The basest reason of all," Frank said. "Once you're rich, it costs a hell of a lot of money to stay rich. And I fully intend to sustain and maintain my status quo."

It wasn't the answer I was expecting.

"You mean she *wasn't* trying to steal and plagiarize your book?"

"Who?"

"The girl. Marisol Alfaro."

Frank smirked.

I thought he might lower the gun, or even put it away and say *"April Fool!"*

Instead, he just tightened his grip, rested the butt of the gun on the table and kept the business end aimed straight at my heart.

"Okay, I was wrong," he said. "You're actually a *worse* detective than I thought. Much worse. Why would she try to plagiarize a book that's already in print and on the best-seller list?"

He had a point. Why, indeed? I had made the classic rookie mistake of assuming I had solved the case. Then I had closed my mind to all other possibilities.

At this point in detective novels, when the grizzled hero is similarly endangered, he –or she – often has something tough, astute or even snarky to say. Then, if you're Spenser, for example, a sudden blast from a shotgun blows the bad guy's head off, and Hawk steps into view, just barely showing a smile.

I could think of nothing at all to snarl, to pontificate upon or even to wisecrack. And there was no cavalry nearby, ready to charge.

I was just very sorry now that I had *not* chosen to study real estate. Or astronomy. Or even refrigeration repair.

"I bet you've wondered," Frank said, "how I can write books so quickly."

"Yes, I have," I said quickly. Anything to grab a few more seconds of life. "It hardly seems humanly possible."

"It's *not* humanly possible," Frank said. "Not without help."

"You don't have a staff. I've never seen anyone helping you."

"Don't need 'em. It's like Wordsworth said. 'The world is too much with us.' The planet is now full of unpublished novels, in all genres and languages – and many of them are posted on the Internet. It's a simple matter to download one, run it through some translation software and change a few names and details here and there. Voila, new book."

Frank relaxed his grip on the .45 but did not change its aim.

"And, with my name on the cover, it'll sell a few million copies no matter how bad it is. Most readers, Er, pay no attention to book reviews."

"Okay," I said, trying to act if I were wrapping up a regular conversation. "I won't tell anybody," I said. "It'll be our secret." I had read these words a hundred times in murder mysteries. I couldn't believe I was now saying them now – and meaning every syllable.

"Outside," Frank said. "I don't want to mess up my house."

"No."

He leaned across the table and pushed the gun against the center of my forehead. *Just as he did with Marisol Alfaro*, I suddenly realized.

"Have it your way," Frank said. "I can always buy a new house. And by the time they find your body, I'll be living somewhere overseas behind a big wall of bribes. Outside."

We walked through his big house and out into the night. Frank kept the gun pressed against my back.

"Where are we going?" I said.

"To you, it won't matter."

"Why did you kill her?" I said, starting to feel desperate. Maybe he really *was* planning to shoot me. "You could have bought her off with a bribe. Or made her the co-author of your next book."

"You really *are* stupid," Frank said, pushing the gun harder, trying to make me move faster. "It wasn't her book."

"Whose was it?"

"Her brother's." Frank laughed but kept bumping the .45 against my spine as we walked. "He was one of those hapless fools who wrote in Esperanto because he thought it contributed to world peace."

"But how did you get it?" I figured if I could keep Frank talking long enough, he would change his mind about shooting me.

Or maybe a meteorite suddenly would streak down and hit him in the head.

"He found out he was dying of liver cancer," Frank said. "So he posted his manuscript on a website. It was a going-away gift for his two hundred followers. Most of those Esperanto Looney Tunes will never read it. I did him a big goddam favor by bringing his book to the attention of the rest of the world."

"Without his name on it."

"A minor technicality."

Dry grass and gravel crunched beneath our feet as we walked.

"You could have just made him the co-author, granted him some fame and paid her some royalties," I said.

"Could have. Didn't. Simple as that."

I felt like we were now in the last scenes of a bad detective novel, except I was supposed to have the upper hand. I was supposed to be holding a gun to the killer's head and listening to his tearful or boastful confession just before I called the cops or blew him away.

I realized now that we were walking toward the big tree near his front fence. His eleven Longhorn that usually clustered there were nowhere in sight.

"You won't get away with this," I said.

"Of course I will," Frank said.

Weirdly, it bothered me that here we were, two writers, speaking like potboiler characters, and I couldn't think of anything better to say.

I halfway expected Frank to say something about "the big sleep" or "sleeping with the fishes" or "concrete shoes."

Instead, he said nothing more until we were standing under the big tree.

"Stop here."

I heard a slight click as Frank loosened the .45's safety.

Now I had just one chance. And it would work only if Frank had forgotten his Marine training and didn't have a round already loaded in the chamber.

I had not learned the defensive move in Navy boot camp. I had merely read about it in a dozen or so detective novels during my now-gone book reviewing career.

If I could spin, grab the .45's slide and hang onto it for dear life, while keeping the barrel aimed away from me...

Frank suddenly moved the gun up from my back and pressed it against the base of my skull.

SNAP!

He *had* forgotten to chamber the first round. Maybe he hadn't been a Marine after all.

"Shit!" he said. He pulled the gun away from my head, ready to move the slide back.

"Skunk!" I yelled.

I had no idea why. It was utterly incongruous to my predicament, yet entirely plausible. We *were*, after all, standing in a rural field. It must have caused Frank to hesitate for a second and look around, because I was able to turn suddenly and grab the .45's slide with both hands.

Frank tried to pull the gun away from me and fire it. But now we were too old guys struggling under the Texas stars, and I was two years younger than him, and I had promised Joan I would be home by ten.

I had every reason to live.

I gripped the gun harder and tried, with both hands, to keep the barrel pointed away from me.

And Frank tried and tried, with both of his hands, to make the gun go off.

As we danced and grunted and cursed in the moonlight, a silly thought occurred to me: This would be the perfect moment for a cattle stampede. Could I make the right whistle or scream and cause Frank's eleven Longhorn to come running? With luck and precise timing, I could push him under their thundering hooves and…

Frank suddenly thrust the .45 toward my face hard enough that the front of the gun bumped my forehead as I tried to duck.

"Ow!" I said, still hanging on.

"Let go!" Frank said.

I tried to kick him in the crotch, but I couldn't get my leg high enough. My foot went between his legs just above his knees.

As I regained my balance, Frank yanked the gun back hard.

Without wanting to, this time I let go.

I stood frozen now, holding my hands out, gripping nothing but air. I assumed I was doomed.

Frank, however, stumbled backward, lost his balance and fell. For every action, there *is* an equal and opposite reaction.

He held the .45 protectively to his chest as he went down. He tried to keep the big gun from hitting the ground. But he still had his finger in the trigger guard. His elbow smashed against an exposed tree root as he landed.

The gun went off right under his chin. The top of his head exploded.

The shot flashed like lightning and echoed like thunder as I held my ridiculous pose. For a moment afterward, I could neither see nor hear.

Then, silence ruled. But only for a second. As my ears stopped ringing, I could hear dogs barking in the distance, seemingly from all directions.

I expected to hear sirens. But gunshots were common in the Hill Country. People frequently shot at skunks, deer, beer cans and road signs. Once in a while, they even shot at each other.

Frank's body twitched for a moment. Then it was still.

There was no reason to reach down and see if he was still alive.

I knew I had left prints on the gun. But as my eyes readjusted to the moon glow, I saw dark blood and gore flowing down the side of Frank's oddly tilted head. It was soaking all over the gun still clenched in his fist under his chin.

Marisol Alfaro's killer had brought justice upon himself. And he had made it look exactly like an Ernest Hemingway suicide.

It *was* the perfect crime. And it was exactly the kind of vengeance that even Holmes and Dr. Watson had shown willingness to accept, particularly in *The Return of Sherlock Holmes*.

I had two choices now. I could go to my car and call 911, but my cell phone's calling record would put me on the investigators' hook.

Or I could go to my car, drive off into the night, and leave Frank's body to the bugs and buzzards.

As I climbed into my car and touched my phone, I realized there was a third choice somewhere between the other two.

Shaking now, I drove west to a convenience store at the intersection of two dark rural roads and pulled up to the pay phone kiosk in the parking lot. Amazingly, it still had equipment. I grabbed the handset with a Kleenex to block my handprints. I could hear a dial tone. I fumbled around in my pocket and found two quarters. I almost slotted them, but I stopped when I remembered: *Fingerprints!* I laid the coins on my thigh and rubbed them on both sides with the Kleenex. Then I lifted them carefully by their serrated edges and dropped them into the coin chute.

Once the coins were in, I looked up at a little placard above the phone. "*Calls to 911 are free*," it said.

I punched the digits, carefully keeping the Kleenex pressed against my fingertip.

"Nine-one-one. What's your emergency?" the operator said.

I gave her my thickest Texas accent. And I didn't exactly lie.

"I just drove past that crazy old writer's ranch. I think his name is Arkansas or Arkaway. Or maybe it's Arkandale. Somethin' like that. Anyway, I heard a gunshot. I think he might have been tryin' to shoot at me. His place is on Farm-to-Market Seven Twenty Eight. I think he was standing out under a big old tree near his front fence when he shot."

"Okay, sir," the operator said. "I'll report it. Please stay on the line – "

"Sorry. Gotta go," I said.

I hung up and looked around. The store had no other customers, and it looked too poor to have a parking lot surveillance camera. The clerk had his back to the door. He was watching an early autumn football game on TV.

I rolled up my window and drove back to town, watching every car that showed up in my rear-view mirror.

With luck, the call would never be traced to me.

Back in my office, I needed and wanted to pour myself a stiff drink. But I had not yet bought any booze to put in my desk. Clearly, I was no Hammer, Spade, nor Marlowe.

I did have one diet Sprite. I had been saving it so I could put it into the little refrigerator I hoped to buy for my office. My hand shook as I popped the Sprite open it. Gradually, I steadied and took a long, warm swallow.

I found a half-eaten bag of peanuts in the desk drawer. I started eating them, hoping I would not inhale one and choke.

As a P.I., I was still a hapless rookie. Maybe I really *should* take some classes in refrigeration repair. Or dental hygiene.

But at least I finally had the right rubber stamp. It had arrived in the morning mail.

I picked it up, touched it to its fresh red inkpad and carefully stamped its single word onto both sides of the Case 002 file folder.

SOLVED.

SIXTY-TWO

In "The Adventure of Charles Augustus Milverton," Sherlock Holmes surreptitiously witnesses the murder of the evil Milverton. Then he deliberately fails to report this fact to Scotland Yard's Inspector Lestrade. Later, the hapless Lestrade comes to Holmes for help in finding Milverton's killer, and the great detective sternly refuses, saying: "…I considered him one of the most dangerous men in London…and…I think there are certain crimes which the law cannot touch, and which therefore, to some extent, justify private revenge."

I was not Sherlock Holmes, and Frank had murdered himself in the process of trying to murder me. But, in Erwin's Law, just as in Sherlock Holmes's, surely there could be cases that the law should not touch, cases that more or less solved themselves.

I truly wanted to take credit for solving the twin mysteries behind Marisol Alfaro's death and Frank Arkandale's enormous productivity. I had *detected*. I *was* a detective. Yet, Texas still had its private investigator statutes. And I had no state license and, at my age, no possibility of getting one.

Joan's Infiniti was parked in its usual spot outside my apartment.

Joan herself was neatly stretched out on my bed, wearing a truly sexy and wicked outfit from

Frederick's. She had fallen asleep reading a paperback copy of *As You Like It*. She was still holding it.

Without waking her, I took a fast shower. Then, wearing just my best cologne, I stretched out beside her and nibbled at her hair and ear until her eyes popped open and the book fell out of her hands.

"This is *exactly* how I like it," I said quietly, into her ear as we moved closer together and kissed.

Later, once she was asleep again, I carefully slid out of bed, found a pair of shorts and sat at my kitchen with a glass of chocolate soymilk.

The truth needed to come out – at least some of it. But how, without implicating me?

Gradually, a plan came to mind.

First, I could mail anonymous letters detailing the basics of Frank's plagiarism to the *Austin Daily Democrat*, the *Austin American-Statesman* and the *New York Times Book Review*. At least one of the publications might investigate and break the story.

As soon as the letters were mailed, I could tell Sgt. Marklin what I had discovered – through *research* – about Marisol Alfaro and her brother's Esperanto novel. I could point Little Paul to its link on the Web and also give him the translated file – still making no mention of the flash drive I had found in the park. Likely Little Paul would just put the information into Marisol Alfaro's case folder and add it to the others stacked up on his desk.

Then, when the news of Frank's literary crimes emerged, I could buy Little Paul a mocha and show him some similarities I had found between Marisol's brother's book and Frank's *High Noon on Neptune*. And I could raise a possibility: *Maybe he had something to do with her death?*

He would be intrigued, of course. But with the Great Recession still forcing state, county and city budget cutbacks, there would be no money to investigate. And Frank had shot himself several miles outside Little Paul's jurisdiction. The county geniuses would *never* figure it out.

Maybe I could convince Little Paul to mail my findings to the El Salvadoran police department that had first investigated Marisol's disappearance. Her parents had lost a son to cancer, as well as a daughter to murder. Perhaps something in my notes or Frank's death would bring them at least a modicum of comfort.

Meanwhile I would not be able to tell Joan *everything*. If she knew the exact extent of what had just happened and how close to death I had blundered, she would immediately have me encased in amber. Or at least insist that I take up astronomy, oil painting or ham radio and never again even *think* the word "detective."

SIXTY-THREE

The next morning, Joan did not have a house showing, so we slept in. To my amazement, I did not dream anything at all about Frank. I woke up when a text message beeped my phone. It was from Big Paul: "The doc says no Big C, just age-enlarged prostate. See you later at Starbucks."

While Joan cooked breakfast, I brought in the newspapers. The *American-Statesman* and the *Daily Democrat* both had front-page stories announcing Frank Arkandale's death.

"…in what appears to be a Hemingway-like suicide," the *Statesman* declared.

"The writer was found lying under a tree amid his small herd of Longhorns," the *Daily Democrat* reported. "'There was no sign of a struggle,' a sheriff's department spokesman said. "The single gunshot appeared to be self-inflicted. We found his body amid a bunch of hoof prints. His cattle apparently walked all over him after he was deceased."

The county geniuses indeed *had* figured it out. Case closed.

"Damn! Frank Arkandale died," I told Joan.

"Your friend?" she said.

"It says here he committed suicide."

Joan looked at the *Daily Democrat*'s report. "That's terrible."

She looked at my face and tried to figure out its expression.

"You went to see him yesterday," she said.

"I did. He was in a very bad mood. Then he had nothing else to say. So I left."

It was, in essence, a truthful summation.

"Are you going to investigate his death?" she said.

"What's to investigate?"

"You're a detective, aren't you? He was your friend."

"Not really."

Joan gave me a quizzical look. She carried the breakfast plates over and set them down on the dining table. She sat down in her chair.

I picked up my fork, ready to start.

"Bacon," I said. "I love bacon."

"Not really a detective? Or not really your friend?"

I leaned over the table, kissed her, and got a spot of strawberry preserves on my shirt sleeve.

"He used to be my friend," I said. "I thought he was, anyway."

"What happened?"

"Apparently I said something he didn't like – about one of his books."

"When?"

"Recently."

"Which one?"

"His newest best-seller, *High Noon on Neptune*. I said it read just like another book I had seen recently."

Once again, I was *not* lying.

"And – ?"

"And, no, I'm not really a detective. I'd like to be one, yes. But I can't. Not officially. Not at my age. And not in this state."

"Do you want to move to another state? Where you don't have to have a license?"

"What, South Dakota? Mississippi? Colorado? You would *hate* Wyoming. This is home. And you know this market. You would have to start all over."

"You can get licensed," Joan said. "You told me there are several ways. If you want a criminal justice degree, I'll help you pay for it."

"I'm too old for that. Anyway, nothing will happen to me if I keep calling myself a private researcher and if I also say I'm writing an article or a detective novel."

"So what will you investigate – what will you *research* – next?"

"I'm very glad you asked that," I said. I got up from my chair, walked around behind her and dug my fingers into her hair. I pulled it apart gently and kissed the back of her neck.

"You," I said. "After breakfast, after bacon, I plan to investigate – I plan to research – you."

"Privately, of course?" she said, looking up at me and smiling.

Somewhere in the universe, a bright star now was rising from behind a mountain. And no doubt princes and princesses were strapping on their sandals and swords, ready to do their epic battles in space.

But here on the good Earth, the muscles in my cheeks merely tightened a bit, until my smile expanded into an unabashed grin.

"Oh, *very* privately, madam, I assure you. My private eyes will be on you alone."

THE END

ABOUT THE AUTHOR

Si Dunn's other books include *DARK SIGNALS*, *JUMP*, and *ANCHORING*. He lives in Austin, Texas.

www.ingramcontent.com/pod-product-compliance
Lightning Source LLC
Chambersburg PA
CBHW070801200626
46811CB00023B/322